APACHERIA

WILLIAM ALTIMARI

IMPERIUM BOOKS

This book is a work of fiction. Any resemblance to actual events or persons, living or dead, is entirely coincidental.

"Apacheria," by William Altimari. ISBN 978-1-60264-251-5 (soft) 978-1-60264-252-2 (hard).

Published 2008 by Virtualbookworm.com Publishing Inc., P.O. Box 9949, College Station, TX 77842, US. ©2008, William Altimari. All rights reserved. No part of this publication may be reproduced, stored in a retrieval system, or transmitted in any form or by any means, electronic, mechanical, recording or otherwise, without the prior written permission of William Altimari.

Manufactured in the United States of America.

For Mo & Kat,
With love
&
In Memory of the American Horse Soldier

THE NATION THAT MAKES A GREAT DISTINCTION
BETWEEN ITS SCHOLARS AND ITS WARRIORS WILL
HAVE ITS THINKING DONE BY COWARDS AND ITS
FIGHTING DONE BY FOOLS.

--Thucydides

1

On the day after my eleventh birthday, he rode into our lives. I was sitting on the hitching rail near my horse in front of mother's mercantile when he came into view. He sat a tall sorrel mare. Many other riders filled the street this Friday morning, but they seemed to melt from my vision when he approached. He paused at a water trough halfway up the street, and his copper colored mount lowered her head. He took in everything around him while his horse refreshed herself. Then he turned her toward the center of the street and nudged her from a walk to a trot. He was not lingering here. He was moving on.

Many eyes observed him, even those of young women who were hooked on their husbands' arms. This was odd, for the rider was no youth. That he was a horse soldier none could doubt, even were it not for the uniform. He sat the horse like a man born to the saddle. And there was a martial quality to his bearing that could never be faked. He wore the usual cavalryman's dark blue wool blouse with the gold shoulder board insignia, along with the wool trousers of sky-blue kersey with the yellow stripe down the side. Black boots extending to the knees protected his lower legs. A buff hat, flat-brimmed with a pinched crown, shielded his head. It was stained with the sweat of countless campaigns. A half-flapped black holster holding a butt-forward revolver nestled against his right hip. I

could see the ivory grips even at this distance. They were an unusual touch for a soldier. A carbine in a saddle scabbard hung beneath his right leg.

I had seen soldiers before, though not so many lately now that most of the Indians had been subdued. So there was no reason for me to notice him. Yet at that moment he seemed to be the most noticeable man on earth. When he came abreast of me, his gaze glided over me. I reached out to Dollar, my bay, hitched to the rail next to me and tried to steady myself. Dollar swished his tail and the summer flies flew off. One buzzed around my nose and tickled me and made me sneeze.

The cavalryman turned and looked. Without thought, I smiled at him.

Mother later insisted it was no fly. She said my guardian angel had fluttered her wings under my nose. I know now that mother was right. Unless you accept the profound wisdom of that, you can understand nothing of what follows.

The soldier laid a rein gently against his horse's neck, and she turned and brought him over to the rail. A saber in a metal scabbard hung under his left leg.

"Good morning," he said.

My lips felt like street dust. "Hello," I managed to say.

He pushed his hat back and smiled.

His hair was as white as bleached muslin and matched the thick moustache drooping over his lip. At the corners of his eyes, the Arizona sun had gouged creases as deep as canyons. Fifty was my guess at his age, though I was a poor judge of things like that. Yet such thoughts occurred to me only later, for now I could focus on nothing but his eyes. Blue does not describe them. I had seen many blue-eyed Irishmen out here. The eyes that gazed at me were aquamarine. As liquid and beautiful as any woman's eyes, and so out of place in that sun-ravaged face.

"A lovely young lady should never be out in this sun without protection." He took the red silk bandana from his neck and draped it over my head and knotted it beneath my chin.

"Thank you, captain," I said.

He smiled again, but this time more to himself than to me.

"Is this what all the cavalry officers wear?"

"No. We wear what we like. I bought that in Tucson."

The look in his eyes puzzled me. He seemed to get such joy in the simple act of placing a bandana around a young girl's head. As if he had so little outlet for these gestures and this was a rare moment. He continued to gaze at me, as if doing so were the most pleasurable thing in the world.

Then I saw his gloved fingers tighten around the reins and he prepared to move off.

"Your canteen is leaking." I pointed at it.

He looked down to where it hung from the saddle. The tan canvas with "U.S." stamped in black was soaked.

"That's odd," he said, a strange look on his face. "I just bought that. Doesn't make sense."

"We sell canteens."

He looked up. "We?"

"My mother and I. This is our mercantile."

I was not sure if I were imagining this, but he seemed pleased with an excuse to linger.

I smiled at him. "I'll trade you one for the bandana."

"Fair deal." He pushed himself up in his stirrups. Then as he looked off to the right, I felt as if a winter wind had hit me. At the moment of dismounting—when a rider is most vulnerable—his eyes changed. They were ice-blue now. He was not gazing down the street between two rows of buildings. He was scanning a gulch between a pair of bluffs that threatened to explode with hostile Apaches. Never before had I felt the weird unease I did at that moment. And never had I felt so utterly and serenely safe.

His right foot touched the ground, and when the left slid from the stirrup he looked down at me, as if to reassure himself that all was still well. His eyes were soft again. Instead of hitching his horse in the usual slovenly cowboy fashion, he tied the reins to the rail in a quick-release knot, what lawmen and the

old alkalis called a bank robber's knot.

He removed his gauntlets and slipped them over his black belt. Then he held out his left hand and smiled. "Show me."

Mother's store was always such a jumble. One of the reasons she had difficulty making a profit was that she held so much stock. We sold just about every houseware and implement you can imagine. Even a field mouse would have been frustrated looking for a nook to take a nap. Other merchants had told her that goods and space are money tied up. Yet that had no effect on her. She felt bad if a farmer or rancher were desperate for something she could not supply. She would hold onto things for years in the chance that someone someday might need it. No matter that it ate into her profits. Yet, as the padre once said, she was surely building up treasures in Heaven.

Mother was seated behind the counter and tending to the books. She wore the high-collared white dress with the pink roses that I liked so much. The dress was as stiff as a sheet of tin. Mother never would wear a dress that was not starched.

The cavalryman's heels on the floorboards and the tinkle of the tiny steel rowels in his brass spurs caused her to look up.

Her puzzled expression was precious as I led the big soldier into the store by the hand.

"You have a fine salesman here, Ma'am. Don't let her go."

Mother had a way of smiling—half-smiling, really, without showing her teeth—that was more striking than a shooting star. Of course, to me she was not simply the loveliest woman in Arizona, she was the Queen of the Earth.

"Good morning, colonel."

He removed his hat. "A very good one, I think."

"How may I help you?"

"He needs a canteen," I blurted out.

"He?" mother said with a stern look. "Is that how you refer to this gentleman?"

I was embarrassed by my rudeness. My face felt like it was on fire. But I did not know his name.

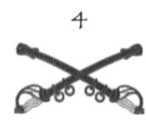

Apacheria

Mother extended her right hand across the counter. "I'm Mrs. Malone."

"Red McGregor," he said and shook it.

I noticed him glance at her ringless left hand.

"And you've met Katy." She looked down at me and the sternness was gone from her eyes.

"I've had that pleasure."

Mother reached to the wall behind the counter to one of the dozen canteens hanging there. It was a full quart size and wrapped in light blue wool for insulation.

"Will this do?"

"More than fine."

"Would you like a bandana to replace that?" mother asked, gesturing to the one on my head and winking at me.

He looked down and smiled. "Some things are irreplaceable, don't you think?"

"Yes, they are," mother said, eyeing me in her own special way.

I had no idea what they were talking about.

The colonel pulled a coin from his watch pocket.

"Mother, I told Colonel McGregor we would trade for the bandana."

"Then a trade it is," mother said.

"I think I'm getting the better of this deal," the colonel answered.

Mother smiled. "Colonel, there are many who would tell you that I'm not the shrewdest businesswoman."

He let his hand drop below the edge of the counter where mother could not see and then slid the coin into my palm.

"Katy, eh? A fine name for a pretty young lass."

I grinned at him. "Thank you, colonel."

"That sounds so formal. Let's make it Mac."

"Colonel, I don't think—," mother began but he held up a hand and she stopped.

That startled me. It was the first time I had ever seen a man

silence mother.

"Agreed?" he said, looking at me.

"Yes, Mac."

Then he turned, reluctantly it seemed, and said to mother, "Mrs. Malone, it has been my very great pleasure."

He put on his hat and made for the door and out of our lives forever.

I spun toward mother. My eyes must have looked frantic.

"Colonel . . . ." mother said.

He turned back.

"Every Friday Katy and I treat ourselves to a meal at the hotel. Would you join us?"

"I'd be honored."

And he meant it. That I could see.

Mother left the store unattended, as she often did. She had an "honor box" on the counter for purchases while she was out. Another drain on her profits, but she never seemed to care.

We went out together onto the boardwalk.

"Mac, I'm sorry . . . ." I said.

"For what?" he said in surprise.

"For calling you captain."

He laughed and immediately set me at ease. It was a gruff laugh, but kindly and warm.

"Well, you're the first person who ever succeeded in demoting me." He tapped a forefinger against the end of my nose. "And believe me, many have tried."

I pulled the bandana backward off my head and wore it down on my neck like a soldier.

He went over to his horse. He loosened the cinch, then spoke to her in a low voice and scratched her withers. The gentle dip of her head and her relaxed lips showed how at ease she was, even in a strange town, as long as Mac was there.

We crossed the crowded street and stepped up to the Paradise Hotel—"Misnamed," mother always said in a gentle jab at the head waiter, though they did have good food.

Apacheria

The dining room was full, but we went to an empty table near a window with a "Reserved" card in the center.

Mac pulled out the seats for mother and me, then hung his hat on the corner of his chair and sat down.

I can barely remember the meal now. Mostly what I recall is staring at Mac the whole time. He was big for a cavalryman. Yet he was trim in the waist, and he moved with a grace rare in large men. Very different from the lumbering farmers I knew. Horsemen truly were a different breed.

He was curious about the crowds, and mother told him that our summer fiesta was about to begin.

"Would you like to stay?" I asked him. "There are dances and games and spicy foods and—."

Mother touched my knee under the table, and I stopped.

"You've been on the trail a long time?" mother said to him.

"Do I look that mossy horned?"

"A little weary, I think."

"I was visiting California. I'm headed back to Fort Huachuca."

"Were you posted to California?" mother asked.

"No. I've been scouting for a place to retire. But California was a bad choice. It's very lush, but I realize now that I prefer harsh beauty to soft beauty." He looked at me and smiled. "Well, most of the time anyway."

I started to say something, but suddenly he was no longer with us. He was staring past mother. Yet he was really turned inward, as though gazing in some uncertain fashion at an unfamiliar map to an unknown land he was about to enter.

Mother reached under the table and squeezed my leg, and I took her hand in mine.

"What day is today?" he asked, coming out of his reverie.

"Friday," mother said, almost in a whisper.

"No, the date."

"The tenth."

He nodded. "I thought so. As of midnight, the United States

Cavalry will have one man less. Officially, Redmond McGregor will be a private citizen."

Mother remained silent. She clearly did not know if she should congratulate him.

"It's been a long journey," he said. "And all journeys must end."

But there was no joy in his voice.

Then mother did something I thought was very forward. She laid a hand on the cuff above his right wrist.

"Why not stay for the fiesta, Mac?"

He smiled, and the creases in his face deepened again into canyons.

I looked at mother. I could not remember seeing her so radiant. Her eyes glittered like emeralds. Mac's smile had ignited a vivacity in her I had not seen in years. Even the sun cooperated. Beams of morning light streamed through the window and lit her pile of auburn hair until it gleamed like a sorrel's coat.

We ate well that day. Steak and eggs, I think, and potatoes and milk and what must have been a pint of black coffee for Mac. We were truly sated when we leaned back in our chairs.

An explosion of hoofbeats caused Mac to swing toward the window. They sounded simply like running horses to me, but he sensed something different—ominous, too, from his intense expression when he peered out.

Amid the shouts, I could make out one word over and over—Manolete.

"What's going on?" Mac asked mother, as if it were the most natural thing in the world for this woman to know.

"Manolete fled the reservation."

"Alone?"

"Supposedly with about a dozen bucks."

"When?"

"We heard about it this morning, but apparently it happened about a week ago."

Mac looked back out the window.

Apacheria

Ten men on horseback seemed to be trying to work up the courage to go after them.

"Who are they?"

"Just locals," mother said. "The talker is called Scabby."

"Because he had a bad case of the pox," I said, but it was hardly the most helpful remark.

Some townspeople had gathered to watch the excitement.

"This is bad," Mac said.

That made no sense to me. Who cared if a makeshift posse tried to run down a few escaped Indians?

Mac turned toward mother. "What kind of peace officer do you have in this town?"

I giggled. "He's sweet on mother."

Her eyes shot arrows at me, and my smile vanished.

"He's a fine man," mother said to Mac.

"He should stop this."

Mac got up and went toward the door.

Leg irons could not have held me to that table. I ran behind Mac out onto the boardwalk. I heard mother follow and expected her to scold me. Instead she just stood behind me and placed her hands on my shoulders.

The riders were growing angrier and cockier by the second.

"Katy," Mac said. "Go get the sheriff."

"I'll do it," mother said.

She slid me closer to Mac and hurried off.

There was no holding them back. The pot was boiling and spilling over. By the time mother returned with Sheriff Blaine, there was no hope. Scabby tossed an indifferent glance at the sheriff, and the horsemen turned and raced away.

Reflexively, Mac hooked a protective arm around me.

"Jim, this is Colonel McGregor," mother said.

"Pleased to meet you," Jim said, and shook Mac's hand, though he did not seem pleased about Mac's arm around my shoulder.

"You're in for a world of trouble, sheriff," Mac said.

"How is that?"

"Don't you know?" Mac seemed stunned.

"It's not against the law for some men to get together and ride out of town."

"Against the law? What does that have to do with it?"

Jim was getting annoyed. "There was no legal force for me to exert."

Mac laughed and it was harsh. "A lawman who relies on legal force is firing wet charges. I'm talking about moral force."

"I suppose you could have stopped them." Jim was angry now.

"A schoolgirl could have stopped them. They were a mob. Easiest thing in the world to break. A rock to the side of the head would have knocked the leader from his saddle, and that would have been the end of it. That was your chance. Now people might die."

The three of us stared at Mac as if he were crazy. What could he be talking about?

"Jim, will you join us for coffee?" mother asked.

He looked like he had swallowed a cholla, but I knew he would take any excuse to spend time with mother.

The waiter had cleared the table and now brought us a fresh pot of coffee. Jim's lean and pleasant face was blank. Mother was waiting for the men to discuss the matter, but the silence was as thick as fresh manure.

Mac sipped his coffee and seemed to be in another world.

"Colonel," mother said at last, "why might people die?"

Mac looked up. "Do you know anything about Manolete?" he said to Jim.

"A little."

"He's the toughest and wisest Apache since Cochise."

"I've heard that. I don't believe it."

"First mistake."

Jim's lips tightened.

"If he left the agency a week ago, do you think he's still in Arizona?" Mac asked.

Apacheria

"Where would he go?"

Mac looked at him as if he were a child. "Mexico. Where else?"

"Why there?" mother asked. "The Mexicans hate the Apaches."

"Because Mexico is the best place to rob and kill Mexicans. And the Apaches do that with gusto. Manolete is down there marauding. Stealing stock and slaughtering Mexicans as he pleases."

"How does that concern us?" Jim asked.

"Jim!" mother said. "That's a terrible thing to say."

"Do you think he'll stay there?" Mac said. "That herd of churn-heads that just rode out of here won't want to come back empty-handed. They'll snatch some pathetic Apache who stole a horse ten years ago. He'll be their trophy. And then hell begins."

"I don't understand," mother said.

"Manolete will hear of it. He'll ride up out of Mexico and sweep across this land like a sheet of flame. Farmers will be afraid to tend their crops. Ranchers will fear for their herds and their lives. Anyone careless enough to stray will be lashed to a wagon wheel and the wagon set on fire." Mac sipped his coffee. "Have you ever heard the screams of a man tied to a burning wagon, sheriff?"

"No."

"I have." He turned and gazed out the window. "Well, I guess we'll be popular again."

I knew exactly what he meant. The only time soldiers were liked was when the Indians were causing trouble. The rest of the time the soldiers were ignored or swindled. Easterners who came west were always surprised when they learned that most soldiers looked at the Indians with respect. It was the whites the soldiers viewed with contempt. The settlers were always throwing kerosene on every ember to arouse the soldiers to wipe out the Indians once and for all. The average rancher or townsman was far more fanatical about the Indians than the

wildest Indian fighter. A simple clerk in a hardware store made the dead Custer look like a Quaker.

"Do you live in town?" Mac asked mother.

"No, a few miles out."

"Can you shoot?"

"Yes."

"Maybe you should stay in town for a spell," Jim said.

"I can't abandon my house and my chickens and my garden. And besides, I can't afford to rent a room."

Mac stared out the window again. "I think I'll stay for the fiesta. Problem is that all the hotels are full."

"You can have my room!" I shouted, before realizing there was no way for Mac to have known that all the rooms were taken.

"Do you think you can squeeze in with me?" mother asked me.

It was obvious what answer she wanted.

"Yes!"

Jim looked like he had bitten off another piece of cholla. Yet he said nothing. Mother's reputation was unassailable.

Mac smiled at me and winked, and then looked at mother. "That sounds more than fine."

2

I was crazy with excitement. I think mother was as well, but she had the special skill of concealing feelings she thought inappropriate at the moment. She was subdued now for Jim's sake. I could see he was worried. Mac's warning about the Apaches had struck its target. Of course, this was a federal matter and not really any business of a small town sheriff. Yet Jim was a conscientious lawman, and Mac's sharp rebuke had drawn blood. Jim was also a sensitive man, which he tried to hide. He was often clumsy at it.

And then there was the presence of Mac himself. I could see that bothered Jim. The light in mother's eyes when she spoke with Mac could not be misread. Jim had long carried a torch for mother. Yet he had always managed to drop it and run for cover. I was not surprised. Mother intimidated most men. The women around town thought it was her beauty and envied and resented her for it. But it had nothing to do with that. Mother could have tied her hair in knots and worn sackcloth and ashes, and still she would have overwhelmed without trying. Her feminine intensity was God's gift to her. She guarded it carefully. But even her propriety could not shield others from the heat of the fires within her. Fires that I, at eleven, was just beginning to feel flickering within myself as well. Teenaged boys became tongue-tied in her presence, even though she was thirty-six years old at the time. Middle-aged men found excuses to make trivial

purchases, sometimes several a day, just to come into our merc. She treated them all with a restrained elegance that only increased their misery. It was not until a few years later, when I had flowered, that I fully realized how she drove them mad.

Mac disappeared after breakfast. Jim went to the telegraph office, and mother returned to the store.

Mexican women were stringing bunting and flowers along the street for the fiesta. Ordinarily I would have joined in. They always were happy to see me and feed me sweets as if I were starving. Today, though, I was distracted and just milled around.

Timmy McCrea distracted me more. He rode up in the wagon from the feed store where he worked after school and on Saturdays. No matter where I was, he always seemed to find me. I was still trying to understand boys. Why could they not just look at girls, instead of gazing at them as if they were in a trance? They always seemed stupefied. Timmy was thirteen and stared at me as if I were the center of his world. I was more interested in horses than boys then, so his attentions annoyed me. Yet they annoyed me less than they used to, but I did not like to think about that. Even so, I would have laughed like a chucklehead if at that moment anyone had told me that someday I would bear his children.

"Hop on, Katy," he said.

"Why?"

"I'm headed to your place."

"What for?"

"To make a delivery."

The three sacks of grain in the wagon could not have been for us. Though our horses needed some fattening up, I knew mother could not afford grain right now.

"Come on," he said with a smile.

"I'm busy."

"All right," he said and rode off.

Regardless of how many times I pushed him away, Timmy never lost his cheerfulness.

For the first time, I felt bad as I watched him ride out.

I went back to the store.

Three men, all with sourpuss wives, had found a reason to discuss with mother the finer points of axe handles as if they were considering the purchase of precious gems.

When Sheriff Jim came in, mother called to me.

"Take the counter, Katy."

Mother and Jim went to the small room behind the counter.

The ranchers quickly concluded their purchases and left with their wives.

I could see the little back room from my perch on the stool. Mother used it to relax with a cup of tea or to teach me arithmetic in spare moments. I knew my numbers better than anyone at school.

I picked up the stool as quietly as I could and moved it closer so I could see better.

"He's not my friend, he's Katy's," mother was saying.

"Katy's?"

"I think her smile was like a little key. It unlocked a part of his heart that he had forgotten about. Or maybe didn't even know was there."

I felt flush when mother said that.

"I think you're being naïve."

Mother's eyes narrowed. I never liked that. And it did not bode well for Jim. He was fumbling the torch again.

I think Jim was waiting for a response, but she just stared at him in silence.

"He's a soldier, Mary. You know what soldiers want."

No! I screamed inside my head. I knew exactly what Jim meant.

"Does he Jim?"

Mother's voice was as pleasant as steel on a whetstone.

"I worry about you and Katy."

"Don't."

I had never heard mother use that tone before, to Jim or to anyone else.

"I'll lend you the money to stay in town until this Indian business blows over."

"Thank you no. I can take care of my daughter and myself."

"People will talk."

"They always talk. When they start making sense, then I'll worry."

My God, how I loved my mother. And admired her like a goddess.

Jim looked away. The torch had sputtered out again.

"I'll see you later," he said and got up.

I spun around on my stool to face the counter. He never noticed me as he hurried out of the store.

I liked Jim. Always had and always would. Yet he seemed shorter today. I had assumed he would marry mother eventually. That no longer seemed sensible.

Mother came up behind me and slid her arms gently around my upper body.

"It's not polite to eavesdrop," she said and kissed me on the top of the head.

I leaned back against her chest and just rested there.

"Mommy, do you like Timmy?"

"Very much."

"He likes me."

"I know."

"I think I was mean to him today. I feel bad."

"Feeling bad about things like that is a sign of growing up."

I did not turn around, but I could hear the smile in her voice.

"We can trust Mac, can't we?" I asked.

"Oh, yes. I'd trust him with my life. More importantly, I'd trust him with your life."

"But why do we feel that?"

"You're too young to know, and I'm too old not to know."

I turned around and rested my face against her breast. I loved the smell of lavender she wore.

"I think he's a little sad."

"Yes," mother said.
"About leaving the army, do you think?"
"Yes, and about losing his wife."
I snapped my head up. "His wife?"
Mother kissed me on the forehead.
"How do you know?"
"The deep groove on his ring finger. It hasn't been long."
"Do you think he has children?"
"No. I'm certain of it."
That puzzled me. "How can you be so sure?"
She smiled and stroked my hair. "I just know."
"He's lonely then?"
"All men are lonely. That's why if their wives die, they die, too. But if husbands die, their widows live on."
"I can't imagine a man like Mac dying."
"Part of him already has. But a new shoot sprouted this morning. Planted by a little girl with auburn hair and the pinkest cheeks ever a man did see."

I slipped my arms around mother and pressed my face to her and just held.
"I want you to be happy, mommy."
"That's a sign of growing up, too."
"I never want this day to end."
"It never will. It's set down roots."
"I'm a little afraid, though. I don't know why."
Mother hugged me very tightly. "I'm a little afraid, too."

Over and over throughout the afternoon, I heard people say, "Time to see the Jew." Mr. Shapiro owned a gun store at the edge of town. He and his wife Esther had lived there since before I was born. His wares had been the difference between life and death for many out here. But to most of them, he was still just "the Jew."

Mr. and Mrs. Shapiro might have been sixty years old or they might have been a hundred. I could never figure out those things. He was round and bald with a fringe of white hair and had rimless spectacles that looked like they had been made from the bottoms of inkwells. The story was that he had been a gunsmith in the Prussian army. He struggled to make himself understood with a Yiddish accent as heavy as cement. Mrs. Shapiro was no taller than a large child and looked to weigh less than one of Mr. Shapiro's revolvers. She spoke little English, but every time she saw me she would yell, "Sam!" He would instantly stop what he was doing and go and pick me some strawberries from his little patch out back. If I were really lucky, he would have some fresh cream to pour over them. One of my earliest memories—I was so young I can see it now only through a sort of gray haze—was Mr. Shapiro bending down toward me and smiling and handing me a tiny bowl of strawberries.

I adored them both. I think that made me unique in town. Except for mother, of course. She had said more than once that she did not understand Jews, she was frank about that. Yet she recognized goodness. When Mrs. Shapiro had burned with a fever that baffled the doctor and scared everyone else, mother sat up all night and sponged her down with alcohol. I stayed in the parlor and played cards with Mr. Shapiro to distract him from his worry. When the fever broke the next morning, we slipped out of the house while they were both asleep. Mother did not wait for thanks. She cared nothing for that. Later that day, Mr. Shapiro, smiling his great smile, showed up at our store and presented mother with a beautifully engraved shotgun. I have it still.

Mother was not simply familiar with firearms, she was a natural. And she knew their value. She had taught me to shoot when I was about eight. I was now pretty good with a short carbine and could pop tins off a fence with a Colt Lightning revolver at twenty paces. Few things irritated mother more than prissy Easterners who came to Arizona and recoiled at the armories on people's walls or hanging from their waists. "Then

go back," she would tell them, without even the pretense of politeness. "To your dirty alleys where thugs will slit your throat in darkness." She was never shy about her opinions. Ironically, mother was an Easterner herself. But she had been born in Gettysburg and was in her early teens at the time of the battle. She said that life was a gift from God but survival was in the hands of man. When I asked her about that once, she told me not to forget that the greatest of the archangels was never to be seen without his sword.

I was sitting at one end of Mr. Shapiro's counter case and gorging on strawberries when Clete Lomaddis came in. He pushed to the front of the group of people lined up to buy cartridges. Those who hesitated he elbowed aside.

Padre Tomas had said that good Catholics do not hate. That was why every time I saw Lomaddis, I went to Confession. But I could not change my feelings. This was not simple dislike. He frightened me and filled me with revulsion. Yet he rarely had an expression other than a smile. But it was not a smile to set you at ease. It was the smile of a man who could pluck a flower and give it to a young girl or reach down and cut the head off a puppy with equal pleasure. It was the grin of a bizarre man who seemed barely sane. When he was in the room, I was almost too afraid to breathe.

He pointed to a '73 Winchester in the case, and Mr. Shapiro pulled it out. It was a fine weapon, only lightly used. Lomaddis opened the action and examined the chamber.

I think it was his eyes I found most disturbing. They were heavy-lidded, and so seemed always about to close. They made an odd combination with that constant smile. The face just did not seem normal, like a portrait by an amateur artist in which the features failed to line up right. And his hair was grotesque. I had never known any other man under sixty who dyed his hair. Lomaddis was younger than mother, but dye it he did. I figured he must have used some kind of henna, because the hair was reddish. It never looked fresh, though. Brown roots always

showed. I could not guess what he saw in the mirror, but it surely could not be what I was looking at now.

"A niiiice pieeeece," he said to Mr. Shapiro.

His high-pitched voice—which I had heard he was self-conscious about—was as annoying as an untuned fiddle string, and the drawn out words always seemed three feet long. The odd thing was that it could not be said to be a drawl. It was widely known that he had grown up in the slums of New York. He had supposedly gone to sea but had jumped ship in San Francisco and made his way to Arizona. Miss Hentz, our schoolteacher, called his manner of speaking "a linguistic perversion," whatever on earth that meant. To me, it was simply another sign of brain disease.

"Priiiice?"

"Zeventy-fife dollars."

"Fair. I'll take it."

Then he tucked the rifle under his arm and walked away. No money had changed hands.

Mr. Shapiro leaned across the counter. "Zir . . . ."

Lomaddis looked around. "What's the problem? You know I'm good for it."

A few toughs in line laughed, and the rest remained silent. No one dared intervene.

Lomaddis turned and walked toward the door.

"Shtop!" Mrs. Shapiro shouted. She had just come out of the back room and was hurrying toward Lomaddis.

Mr. Shapiro shot out an arm sideways and stopped her.

Lomaddis went out the door and was gone.

This afternoon I would have to go to Confession again.

Mrs. Shapiro was gibbering wildly in Yiddish, but Mr. Shapiro held up a hand for silence. Like all Jews, he knew that he survived only at the pleasure of stronger and crueler men than he. So he went back to selling cartridges as if nothing had happened.

I got up from my stool and went over next to him and gave him a hug. He smiled at me and his thick fingers caressed my

cheek. If the Jewish man I worshipped was the Son of God, as I firmly believed, then this sweet old man was surely worthy to be His cousin.

3

Mother closed the store in mid-afternoon, a rare concession. She wanted to go home early and get us cleaned up so we could come back for the start of the fiesta in the evening. We usually came to town every morning in our buckboard, but today we rode our own horses to be quicker on the way back.

I was full of the story of Lomaddis but could not tell mother during our trot home. When we got there, something was amiss, but in a good way. Everything seemed neater. A fork had been taken to the manure in the corral, old hay had been cleaned up, and the water troughs topped off. A small portion of the corral had been roped off to provide a separate space for Mac's horse, and she munched contentedly on a flake of alfalfa.

The white boards of the front porch had been swept, the chickens fed, and when I dismounted and checked the barn I saw that the stalls were spotless. I was embarrassed by that. The barn was my job, and I had never cleaned it half as well. Three sacks of grain had been stacked outside one of the stalls next to Mac's gear.

Mother and I led our horses to the corral. She removed the tack from her palomino, and I noticed a soft smile on her face. It was not for me. She was half turned away and I just barely glimpsed it.

When we went up to the house, I saw smoke coming from the stove chimney. It had never occurred to me before that in the

army, a world with few women, men had to learn to do "women's work." Even more surprising was that they could do it with relish and do it well.

The smell of coffee greeted us at the door. Somehow the inside of the house seemed different, too, but I could not figure out what it was.

Mac had a cup of coffee in his hand and was examining a cabinet photograph of my father on the mantelpiece. Mac had changed into a spare pair of trousers and a blue bib shirt, what the oldtimers called a fireman's shirt. His hair was damp and combed back.

"Katy has her mother's eyes but her father's chin." He turned to me with a smile. "The best of all worlds, don't you think, young lady?"

"Yes," I said uncertainly and reached out for mother's hand.

"Thanks so much for all you've done. This place is never as tidy as I'd like."

"All I've done?" he said with a laugh. "Very little. Any private in my regiment could have run through it with an arm in a sling. And anyway, a boarder has to earn his keep."

"Don't consider yourself a boarder here."

It was an odd thing for mother to say, and I think she realized it. She averted her eyes and handed me her riding gloves.

"Tell Timmy when you see him that I didn't order that grain."

"I bought it," Mac said. "Your horses can use a few pounds. Consider it my first month's rent."

Month! Was he really going to stay that long?

"Oh, Mac . . . thank you."

Winter had been rougher than usual. It rarely got too cold along the San Pedro River valley, but it had been cool this winter. More to the point, mother's profits had been down at the store. One would think they would stay more or less the same, since people always needed staples, but it never worked out that

way. Mother had had a difficult time paying just the hay bill. Sacks of grain had been a luxury. I knew for a fact that she had skimped on her own meals to buy feed for the horses.

Mother insisted on a bath for me instead of a quick wash up. She took a leisurely one herself. That was significant. She always said that her only private place was the bathtub. I knew that the longer her bath, the more thoughtful or pensive she was. She must have been thinking volumes this afternoon.

Mac and I played poker for matchsticks at the kitchen table while we waited. I saw him examining the intricate woodwork of the tabletop.

"My daddy was a carpenter," I said.

"Mmmmm," he answered and went back to studying the cards in his hand. He clearly would never pry.

"He died when I was two. He cut himself shaving and the wound festered and he got blood poisoning and died."

"I see."

"Mother raised me alone."

"She's a remarkable mother."

"She's gold."

Mac laughed. "That, too."

"She's had many suitors," I said without prompting.

"But none stayed...."

"I guess they were ill-suited," I said with a giggle.

Mac laid down his cards and placed one hand over the other on the table. His open expression encouraged me to continue.

"Some were very nice, but she ended up pushing them all away."

He gazed at me in silence.

"I think it was because she thought none of them would make a good father. She didn't want to risk a bad stepfather with me."

"That shows how much she loves you."

"I know."

And how extraordinary that realization seemed to me now. Mother was off in another room while a strange and powerful

man sat within arm's reach of her daughter who was just beginning to bud.

"Will you come with us to the fiesta?"

"Of course. I wouldn't let you and your mother come home in the dark."

"Oh, Sheriff Blaine would have—." I stopped suddenly and looked down at my cards.

"I hope I didn't squeeze him out for the evening."

"Oh, no. They had a spat this afternoon anyway."

"I'm sorry to hear that. He looks like he cares for your mother."

That seemed irrelevant to me now.

"I suspect there aren't many who are comfortable being your mother's friend."

How could he know that?

"Most women envy my mom. And most men are"—I felt myself blushing—"They feel things when she's near. Things they're ashamed of."

"I understand."

Mac had such a way of soothing me.

"She likes men friends, though. More than women, I think. She says they're more honest with her."

"I suspect your mother sees into people very well."

"She reads my mind!"

"How does that hand read?" He gestured at my cards.

I smiled. "It's a winner."

"Call."

I laid down my hand. "Three kings."

"Four deuces." He fanned the cards on the table in front of him.

"I need more practice."

Mac pulled the pile of matchsticks toward him. He put one in the corner of his mouth and picked up the rest and put them back into the blue and white clay match striker.

"Katy, why doesn't your mother have help here?"

"We can't afford it."

"It wouldn't cost much. Hired hands come cheap."

"But it's still more than we have."

"It would be even cheaper if your mother let him live here. Sleep in the barn or build a shed out back."

I had no answer for that. I really did not know.

Mac shifted his weight in the chair a bit and leaned back. He rolled the match from one corner of his mouth to the other and gazed beyond me. Then he said something I will never forget, though I could not fully understand it at the time.

"The life we're living seems so hard and complicated, but later we look back on it and we long for it because now it seems so simple and secure."

He smiled in a half-sad kind of way. I wanted to touch his hand, but I was afraid to. Then he looked back at me and his eyes were happy again. I could not grasp why he got such pleasure just from looking at me. It was not until long after, when I had learned what horrors those eyes had seen, that I began to understand.

I heard mother from behind me as she came into the room. Before I could turn, I looked up at Mac. His eyes told me what I would see. He took the match out of his mouth. I slid around on my seat and just stared at mother and smiled. She was breathtaking.

A burgundy satin dress I had not seen in years swirled around her like a sheet of dark flame. How it enhanced her own subdued fire. She would be instantly envied by all the women in town and hated by at least half of them.

Mac stood up as she entered the room.

"Mrs. Malone, you look more than fine. I will be honored...."

He inclined his head in a bow.

"Why, colonel, I thank you," she said and gave him a smile and a royal nod.

Adults could be so strange sometimes.

Stunning though mother was, this would not be a lopsided pair. Mac loomed there like a mountain with a snow-capped

peak. The dark shirt and sky-blue trousers did what they always did—made the American soldier the handsomest man on earth. His desert-seared face distracted attention from the compassionate eyes I had seen close up. He stood there starkly in the half-light, a solitary and unassailable figure. Empty of posturing or pretense, here was a man rendered down to an utterly irreducible maleness. He would have made a grand Roman.

Mac turned away from mother, as though he thought he had looked at her too long. He went over to the hearth where his gunbelt lay coiled up and his Springfield and saber in their scabbards stood against the cold fireplace.

"Will you bring your saber, Mac?" I asked.

He turned and said with a serious face, "Do you think I'll need it?"

"No," I said, giggling. "I mean for show."

He glanced at mother and winked at me. "I think the show will be elsewhere tonight. But I'll put the carbine in the buckboard."

Carbine!

"I forgot!" I spun toward mother. "Sit! Sit! Sit! I have to tell you."

Mother adjusted her dress so she would not wrinkle it and sat beside me. Mac sat across.

"Lomaddis stole a rifle from Mr. Shapiro today."

"Stole? How do you know?"

"I saw it!"

I told her the whole story.

"Nobody went for the sheriff?" mother asked.

"I think they were afraid to."

"So he just walked out with it?"

"Like it was his."

"That roach. I'll talk with Jim."

Suddenly I was afraid for mother. I turned to Mac. His expression was as blank as granite.

"Would you like a suggestion?" he asked.

Mother looked at him.

"Let it cool."

"I'll do no such thing. This has to be dealt with."

I worshipped mother, but now she seemed silly second-guessing this seasoned Indian fighter.

"If Shapiro had wanted the sheriff, he'd have gotten the sheriff," Mac said.

Mother hated to be contradicted. Yet the annoyance in her eyes was lost on Mac. I could not tell if he even noticed it.

"All right. But that man is vile."

I stared at mother in amazement. I had never known her to reverse herself like that.

Mac looked at me. "Is he still dyeing his hair red?"

"You know him?!" I shouted.

"Oh yes. He's shed his dander in my direction once or twice."

"He's scary," I said.

"A few years ago he worked for the beef broker who supplied meat to the Apaches at the agency. Foul and rancid slop for top government dollars. The two of them carried away the profits in sacks."

"And people wonder why the Indians flee the reservation," mother said.

"Stupid, isn't it?" Mac said. "Trashy trade goods, rotten meat, degraded lives. Who would want to leave that paradise?"

"Is that why Manolete fled?" I asked.

"Only Manolete knows that," Mac answered.

"I'd like to meet him someday," I said with a little girl's naïveté.

"Pray you never do unless there's a gun to his head," Mac said very softly, his voice as gentle as a priest's. He looked at mother. "He's a towering figure in a towering time. Cunning beyond comprehension and wise to the follies of man. He's ruthless in ways that would stagger the sane. And he's armored

Apacheria

with a savage honor that cannot be bought. Beaten and killed, maybe, but never conquered."

Mother was staring at Mac as intensely as I had ever seen her stare at anyone.

"You've met him. . . ." she said. It was a statement of certainty.

"Yes."

Mac's eyes made me uneasy. He had been sharing with us selected pages from the story of his life, and he had seemed pleased to do that. But now mother had pressed a finger deep into that volume and seemed ready to try to flip it open. His eyes asked her not to.

She slid her finger out. "I'm happy you're with us. Will you stay until this business is settled?"

His eyes softened as he glanced from mother to me. "Is there a man alive who could say no?"

I had never felt safer than when I had snuggled up into mother's arms—never until tonight.

4

Town was lit up like daylight. Lanterns and torches sputtered and crackled down the main street. The music was wonderful. Southerners pounding banjos and Mexicans strumming guitars fought to dominate one another and the evening breeze. Even a few valiant Italians with violins played their airs along the streets as sweetly as if they stood in an opera house.

Fiesta was the one time when mother allowed me to eat whatever I wanted. I quickly devoured a delicious tamale, but that was really just for cover. After it, I descended on the Indian fry bread sprinkled with powdered sugar and then on to sopapillas dipped in honey. Because I spoke Spanish, the Mexican ladies always gave me extra. I was stuffed within fifteen minutes of getting to town.

I was old enough to be on my own, and mother and Mac had disappeared before I realized it. I saw Timmy wandering along the street alone. He spotted me, but this time I did not run away. I went over to him and offered him a sopapilla from my sticky fingers. He looked stunned and held it like it was sacred.

"Eat, silly," I said.

He grinned and popped it into his mouth.

"What's that from?" I pointed to a little swollen bruise underneath his left eye.

"Nothing. Let's get some more treats."

Apacheria

We went to one of the tables set up in the street and bought some fry bread hot from the manteca and wrapped in brown paper. We found a corner of the boardwalk away from the street lamps and sat together in the shadows.

Timmy always looked a little threadbare. He had no real home. His parents had been butchered by the Apaches, and he lived in the loft above the livery stable. Mr. and Mrs. Olvis, who owned the business, did for him what they could, but they had their own big brood to care for.

Timmy worked more than any boy I had ever known—harder than most adults, too. Yet he never seemed to spend any money. He had his own account at the bank, and his earnings went there. His last new footwear was a pair of boots mother had given him at Christmas. Mother explained to me that his bank account was all he had to cling to, so I should not judge if it sometimes seemed that his clothes were falling off him.

He sat happily eating the greasy bread, as if being beside me were a greater thrill than anything at the fiesta. His wants were so simple. Somehow I felt closer to him tonight than I ever had before.

He heard the horses before I did. He looked past me up the street.

"It's Scabby. The posse is back."

They thundered down the street in a demonstration of their own importance. People scattered out of the way.

In the center of the horsemen, two Indians rode with their wrists bound to their saddle horns.

"Looks like they got a couple of them," Timmy said.

The riders pulled up in the middle of town to show off their trophies. The Indians were only fifteen or sixteen years old and looked terrified.

Sheriff Blaine must have heard the commotion, because he showed up quickly. He looked tired. And he was unarmed.

"Quiet!" Jim shouted.

What had been a noisy and festive street a few minutes ago

was now a graveyard, except for the snorting of the horses.

"This is kidnapping," Jim said to Scabby. "Unless you've got a damn good reason for this."

"Citizen's arrest," Scabby shouted to him from horseback.

"On what charge?"

"What are you, a lawyer?"

"No, but I'm the law and you're all fools. Stand aside."

Jim walked up to Scabby and pulled a folding knife from a vest pocket.

Scabby stayed where he was.

Jim opened the blade. "If I nick your horse with this, you're going up and out of the hurricane deck with a thousand pounds of horse on top of you." He looked Scabby dead in the eye. "Move!"

Scabby reined his horse aside.

Jim walked past the riders and up to the Apaches. He sliced the thongs on their wrists, but they kept their hands on their saddle horns, as though fearing a trick.

"Do you speak English?"

They just stared at him.

Jim gestured for them to dismount, but they stayed frozen to their saddles.

"A little public flogging will do them a world of good," Scabby said.

"For what?"

"Theft."

"Of what?"

"Grain."

"What? Are you crazy?"

"We found them helping themselves to barley at old man Devlin's place."

"You're an idiot." Jim turned to the Indians. "Come on, get off those goddam horses."

Scabby kept his right hand away from his sidearm, but I saw his left slide toward the knife on his other hip.

"You can't be that stupid," a voice said from the shadows.

I could have leaped for joy when Mac stepped into the torchlight. He strolled to the center of the street as if this were just a lazy Sunday afternoon.

I looked for mother. She was standing by a post in front of the feed store and smiling proudly at the two unarmed men facing the mob.

"Don't you understand English?" Mac said to Scabby. "Out of the way."

Scabby pulled his horse farther over.

Mac spoke to the two Apaches in their own language, and they immediately slid from their mounts.

"What are you doing?" Scabby asked Jim.

"Overlooking a kidnapping charge. Now all of you get back to your families. Forget about this. Enjoy the fiesta. If I have to speak to you again, it'll be with a ten-gauge."

Jim led each of the Indians by an arm toward the jail. Mac and mother followed.

"Bye, Timmy," I said and bolted after them.

Our jail was used for little more than the occasional drunk. It had a fair sized office with an ancient desk, a gun rack holding some longarms, an iron stove, and some chairs spread around the place. A strap-steel cell was hidden from view in back. Jim lived upstairs.

The Indians headed toward the back, but Jim pushed them at the chairs.

"Tell them to relax" he said.

Mac's gentle voice calmed them and they sat.

They were clothed in white man's rags that even a bum would have thrown away. And they were barefoot.

Mac spoke with them and they talked to him almost eagerly.

In the midst of the conversation, mother left without saying anything.

"They're not even from around here," Mac said to Jim. "They fled Sonora ahead of some Mexican scalphunters. They've never met Manolete."

"Can you believe them?"

"Apaches are too arrogant to be good liars."

Mother soon came back with a large plate of food and handed it to the older of the two Indians. It almost made me cry to see how grateful they were. They dived into the meal.

"Ask them if they know the whereabouts of Manolete," Jim said.

Mac questioned them.

"They heard he's still in Sonora," Mac said. "They were making their way up here to San Carlos where they have some friends among the Coyoteros."

Jim sat on the edge of his desk and studied the Indians while they ate. This was Jim at his best, calm and unexcitable. It was what made him a fine town sheriff.

"Katy, go get Timmy and tell him to bring two twenty dollar horses to the back of the jail."

"I'll do it," mother said.

"Make sure he writes out a bill of sale to me," Jim said. "And do you think you can run over to your store, Mary, and get something for these poor wretches to wear? It's going to be chilly tonight."

Mother smiled. "Of course." She hurried off.

"We'll get them on the road tonight," Jim said to Mac.

He went over to his warm stove and poured some coffee for them.

"You know, colonel, I've never asked God for much. I figure that'll look good on Judgment Day. But one of these days I'm going to ask Him to grant me the privilege of smashing the face of that pock-marked bastard." He turned quickly to me. "Sorry, Katy."

But I barely heard his apology. I was too happy basking in the glow of my two heroes.

Mac smiled and walked over and laid a hand on Jim's shoulder. "Sheriff, even if it lands you a month in Purgatory, it'll be worth the rent."

Jim burst out laughing. "Thanks for being there tonight."

Apacheria

"A trifle."

"It's the trifles that pave the streets of our lives."

"Well, well," Mac laughed. "A philosopher/sheriff. Didn't Plato write about them?"

"I never had very much in the way of the Classics."

"You've missed a great deal. Latin and Greek are the twin roads to happiness."

"Where are you from, Mac?"

"Philadelphia."

Jim nodded to himself, and then looked over at me. "Some fiesta, eh, Katy?"

"It's been wonderful," I said sincerely.

When mother came back with an armful of clothes, the Indians stared at her in disbelief.

"Timmy is out back," Mother said. She set down the clothing.

"Mac, take them into the other room to get them changed and explain everything. I want them out of here before Scabby and the little scabs get any more ideas."

Mac led them back. They were still stuffing themselves as they went.

Timmy came in and handed Jim the bill of sale. Jim looked it over and wrote something on it. Then he went to his desk and pulled out a green metal box. He took some cash from it and handed it to Timmy.

"How's the eye?" Jim asked him.

"Fine," he said and blushed and turned away from me.

Jim pulled a coin from a vest pocket. "For your trouble. Fatten up that bank account."

"Thank you, sir." He looked at me quickly and hurried out the back way.

After the Indians had changed their clothes and come back in, Mac pointed them to the rear door.

"I'll get them on their way," Jim said. "Be back in a few minutes."

Mac threw his hat on a clothes pole and poured some coffee for mother and even a small cup for me. Then he sat on the corner of the desk and sipped his own. He seemed lost in his thoughts.

"Timmy is a good boy," mother said to me. "He didn't hesitate to help." She smiled. "It's nice to have an admirer like that. Especially one who is willing to fight for you."

That puzzled me. "Fight?"

"The bruise on his face. That was for you. I thought you knew."

"No!"

"I heard some of the boys talking about it out on the street. They said one of their little gang made a remark about you and Timmy didn't like it."

"Who?"

"One of them said it was Billy Boy Scarns."

"What did he say?"

"That Katy was a tomboy." Mother rubbed my arm in a comforting way. "That she didn't like boys but wanted to *be* a boy."

"And Timmy hit him?"

"More than once, I was told. I don't know who threw the first punch. Timmy was caught under the eye, I guess, but Billy Boy had to be helped off the street by his friends. They said his mouth was so swollen it looked like a purple cabbage."

I was speechless. I looked at Mac, who was listening to this in silence. He set down his cup and crooked a finger at me. I went over and he pointed to a spot on the desk. I pushed myself up and sat next to him.

"Querida, I want you to remember something. The luckiest girl in the world is the one who has a boy willing to take a blow for her. Don't let him go."

Suddenly I felt my lower lip begin quivering and hot tears fill my eyes. I reached across and threw my arms around Mac's neck. I started crying and did not care who saw me. I was still holding onto him when Jim came back in.

"Everything all right?"

"It's fine," Mac said. "Just a girl problem." He whispered in my ear, "Not a tomboy problem."

I pushed myself up, laughing through my tears. "Never leave us, Mac," I whispered.

I glanced over at mother. Maybe it was just my weepy vision, but I thought her eyes looked misty, too. She turned away.

"You're a lucky man, colonel," Jim said.

"You have no idea...."

"Yes I do."

I sniffed and wiped my eyes.

Jim sat down behind his desk. "We were supposed to have a visitor today, but I guess he's not going to make it. I wired the fort and told them you were here and what you said about Manolete retaliating. They wired back that they'd send an officer to talk with me. He was supposed to be here by now. Maybe we'll see him tomorrow."

Mac smiled at the mention of one of his old comrades coming in. "Fire up another pot of black jack, sheriff. He'll be here tonight."

"How do you know?" mother asked.

"Because he's one of my soldiers and he said he'll be here."

Mother dumped the old coffee and began brewing a pot of fresh.

"He might need food," I said.

Jim gave me some money from the box. "Take the tray, Katy, and get him a nice selection."

That was what I wanted to hear, but not for the reason Jim thought. I grabbed the tray and ran outside.

I looked for Timmy all over, but he had vanished. I wanted to see him so bad. The main street was jammed, and it was hopeless. I filled up the tray with plenty of good things and headed back. Then my angel must have whispered in my ear. I avoided the crowds and went to where we had sat together in

the dark on the corner of the boardwalk.

There he was, sitting alone. He was waiting there in the uncrushable hope that I began to realize was so much a part of him. He stood up as soon as he saw me. All of a sudden, I was so nervous my legs started shaking.

He smiled at me.

"I'm going to be busy the rest of the night," I said.

"I understand."

Though he was two years older than I, I was almost as tall as he was.

"Will you hold this?" I said, giving him the tray.

He took it without asking why.

I pressed my fingers against the outsides of my legs to stop my hands from trembling. Then I leaned forward and kissed him gently on his bruised eye.

"Thank you," I whispered.

Before he could speak, I grabbed the tray and hurried away.

A sweaty cavalry mount hitched to the rail outside the jail told me the soldier had arrived.

When I went into the office, everyone was deep in conversation. Yet the officer immediately stood up and greeted me.

I almost dropped the tray. He was the handsomest man I had ever seen. Though he was covered with trail dust, he looked like one of those dashing black-haired actors in the cartes de visite the photography studios sold.

"Captain Colton," Mac said, "Miss Katy Malone, honorary corporal in the regiment."

"Corporal?" he said. "She's risen quickly."

"The army isn't always fast to recognize talent," Mac said, "but sometimes it stumbles on it in the most unlikely places."

The captain studied me seriously. "Sharp. Attentive. Posture is good." Then he could not help smiling. "And I like the bandana. Welcome to the regiment, Malone."

"Thank you, sir." I offered him the tray. "I brought you this."

Apacheria

He took it and set it on the edge of Jim's desk. "Thank you, Malone. Very thoughtful."

I glanced at mother. She was beaming.

The captain sat back down

"So what do you think, Wade?" Mac asked.

"Hard to say, sir. We haven't heard much about him since he rode south. Sergeant Martinez has some contacts in Sonora. I think he has a few cousins in the *rurales*. All he's heard is that Manolete has stolen food and stock. No killings so far."

"Unusual for him," Mac said.

"Very," Colton answered and looked at Jim. "He chews up Mexicans like beef jerky."

I went over to mother and sat on her knee, though really I was too big for that.

"What does Hargrave think?" Mac asked.

"He agrees with you, sir. We could be in for one hell of a . . . I mean a bad summer."

"So how's my successor doing?"

Colton sighed. "Colonel Hargrave has his moments, sir."

"Give him some time."

Colton shook his head. "He just doesn't have the knack, sir. He's not a born leader, that's certain. He pushes when he should just listen, and he listens when he should push hard. I don't know how he's gotten as far as he has."

"The army always rewards endurance. You know that."

"Sir, it's like when we're growing up and we have a friend who's just a little bit off. Someone who can run, but not too fast. Who can climb trees but usually slips and falls. That's the colonel with the men. He tries hard and he means well, but he always manages to step on a rake."

Colton skipped the tamales and went right to the sopapillas and washed them down with the Arbuckle's.

Mac leaned back in his chair with his coffee and thought for a while.

Jim went to the stove for the pot and refilled Colton's cup.

"Does Hargrave have you do much drilling?" Mac asked.

"No, sir. He's usually not too demanding about that. Unless he gets a gnat up his . . . unless he's upset about something."

"Good. Tell him my suggestion is daily scouts. Check the outlying farms and ranches. Watch the river as carefully as if you're looking for scorpions at midnight. One thing you can be sure of—you can take it to the bank—if Manolete leaves Sonora, he'll ride up the San Pedro."

"I'll tell him, sir."

"It's important that the soldiers keep the settlers calm. We can't have roving packs of nitwits like we had today. The whites should stay alert but not act crazy. When I was a young soldier, my first colonel out here—McCormick by name—told me something I've never lost. 'McGregor,' he said in that great brogue, 'never forget the desert is dry, so it takes just a spark.' He wasn't talking about brushfires."

Colton nodded and sipped his coffee. "We miss you, colonel."

"And I miss the men."

"We had a big mustering out party planned for you, sir. Enough rotgut whiskey to dissolve an anvil. But you never showed."

"Sorry. I had no idea. Anyway, I had much more important business here."

I squeezed mother's hand when Mac said that.

"There's still room for you, you know, colonel," the captain said. "Sieber is always looking for seasoned scouts."

"Sieber?" Mac said, almost choking on his coffee. "I don't think I'd make a good love match with that cranky Dutchman."

"Well, the job is there if you want it, sir. When you're done here."

I squeezed mother's hand more tightly.

"For the future, I mean, colonel," Colton added.

"Ah, the future," Mac said, looking down into his cup and swirling his coffee around. "That terrible Circe who never

delivers on her word." He looked up at Colton. "The future is an illusion. It never arrives. So why think about it—ever?"

Colton just stared at Mac and remained silent.

"Stay with us tonight, Wade," Mac said. "I don't want you on the road tonight."

"You don't want, colonel?" Colton said in a bantering tone. "You're not my superior anymore."

"No, but I'm Red McGregor, and I've kept you alive . . . how many years has it been?"

Colton suddenly looked serious. "Many, sir." The affection in his eyes was there for all to see.

Mac went over and laid a hand on the captain's shoulder. "It's been a long journey, hasn't it?"

"Yes, sir."

"And now it's the Apaches again. Who would have thought? We've beaten them in the field, given them some wonderful diseases, let them live on a few scraps of their own land, and allowed them the privilege of dining on rotten beef. And yet here we are tonight—again—talking and worrying about the Apaches. And do you know why? Because when an Apache leaps on his pony, he's still what he's always been—lord of the desert."

Mac turned and looked toward the window. It was shuttered, but he gazed at it as if he could see out. He just stood there, staring. No one spoke. I think everyone was afraid to.

Finally he said, "That's why a hundred years from now people will still be writing about these times. And why they'll speak with awe and reverence of this savage land. And why they'll call it then what we call it now, what people will call it for all God's time—Apacheria."

5

Never had I been so tired as I was that night. I fell asleep across mother's lap on the way home. Mac drove the buckboard, his rifle always within reach. Captain Colton stayed in town with Jim.

When we arrived home, all I could think of was bed. Mac said he would sleep in the barn, but mother would have none of that. Neither would I. We got my nightshirt from my room and mother helped me undress by her bed. She let me get by without a wash-up. I dropped onto the mattress and barely remember touching the pillow.

Strange dreams flooded me all night. Indians and horses and men in blue. My sleep seemed more exhausting than my day, and it had been the most eventful day of my life. I woke up often and could hear mother and Mac speaking in low tones in our little parlor. Several times I heard "Katy," and it was usually Mac who said it. I liked hearing him speak my name.

Sometime during the night I woke up and saw mother sitting beside me on the bed. She was looking down at me and smiling. I reached out and touched her leg. I had rarely seen her so at ease. Our life had never been simple, and she often seemed anxious. She could not always hide it from me. Now, though, she was as relaxed as a kitten curled up by the fireside. I was so happy to see her this way. And she was more beautiful than ever.

Apacheria

"I love you, mommy," I said.

She reached down and stroked my hair. "God loves us both, Scamp."

I fell asleep with her hand still touching me.

I woke up with the sun in my eyes and the smell of bacon in my nose. I jumped out of bed, brushed my teeth, cleaned up at the washstand, and quickly put on the clothes mother had laid out for me.

She was standing at the little stove. I was surprised how hungry I was considering all I had eaten the night before.

"Where's Mac?"

My voice must have sounded strange.

"What's wrong?" mother asked.

I went over and put an arm around her and just leaned against her. "I had a bad dream."

She set down the spatula. "Do you want to tell me?"

"Mac was lost and I was calling for him to show him the way in the dark but I couldn't find him. I just kept stumbling and falling."

Mother curled a finger under my chin and kissed me on the forehead. "He's feeding the horses."

I heard the door open and saw him coming in.

"Good morning, Katherine."

That startled me. No one called me that except mother when she was angry enough to spit fire. But coming from Mac now it sounded so elegant.

"Good morning, colonel," I said teasingly.

Fiesta marked the end of the school year, so now I had the whole summer ahead of me. Marauding Indians were forgotten as I looked forward to the months ahead.

The three of us ate breakfast and chatted and laughed as though we had known each other forever.

I was disappointed when Mac said he had business in Tucson and asked mother if any of the banks had Saturday hours. I knew that the round trip would take all day. He

promised to be back by nightfall.

Mother read my mind again. "That's fine," she said before I could ask to go with him. "Katy has some cleaning to do."

So much for my first day of vacation.

When we had finished eating, he got ready to go.

"Is that loaded?" he asked, pointing to Mr. Shapiro's shotgun over the mantelpiece.

"No," mother said.

"Load it."

He buckled on his gunbelt. "Querida, will you go give Reba a good currying and tack her up for me?"

"I will."

Mother took Mac's canteen from the peg by the door and filled it up with fresh water from the pitcher.

"See you soon," she said, handing it to him.

"Before the moon rises." He took the canteen. "Thank you, Mary."

Why was it that when Mac said a girl's name it was not simply a commonplace but sounded like a blessing?

That Saturday was the longest day of my life. Mother gave me a list of cleaning chores a whole regiment could not have accomplished in a week. But they did keep me busy, which was good.

Around mid-morning, Captain Colton showed up.

He looked magnificent. Never before could there have been a man who so embodied a young girl's fantasy of a cavalry officer. He would have been mine, too, the day before yesterday.

I was soaked with sweat after having given the water troughs a good scrubbing. I was embarrassed at how I must have looked. Yet he did not seem to notice.

"Good morning, corporal," he said with a grin as he approached on his bay gelding.

"Good morning, captain."

"Is your mother in town?"

"No, she closes our merc on fiesta weekend."

Apacheria

"Captain!" mother said, coming out onto the porch and drying her hands on her apron. "Welcome."

"Ma'am," he said and touched the brim of his hat.

"Are you in a hurry?"

"I fear my colonel pines for my presence."

Mother laughed. "Why not rest your horse and stay for some refreshment? Katy . . . ." She pointed and I hurried over to him.

He swung out of the saddle and handed me the reins.

Mother and Colton went inside, while I tended to his mount. I took him to a trough for a drink and then loosened the cinch and hitched him to the fence with a quick-release knot as Mac would have done. Then I rushed inside.

We still had some fresh biscuits from the morning, and mother was brewing another pot of coffee.

The captain was sitting at the little table where Mac and I had played cards. He was enjoying a cool glass of water while mother put some biscuits and a tub of strawberry jam on a plate.

"This is very kind of you, Ma'am."

"Don't fool yourself," mother said. "I'm demanding payment."

She set the biscuits and a fresh cup of coffee in front of him and then sat down at the table. I took a chair and sat between them.

"Now," she said, "tell me about Colonel McGregor."

It was a command only a very brave man would dare ignore.

"About?" he asked. "How do you mean?"

"I mean everything."

Colton sipped his coffee and eyed mother carefully. "You wouldn't have me betray any confidences, would you, Ma'am?"

I would have! My little-girl conscience would have excused anything if it meant I could learn more about Mac. And if for some reason my conscience did not cooperate, I would beat it into submission until it did.

"Of course not," mother said.

"We served together about eight years. Most of what I'm capable of learning about being a soldier—most of the best things anyway—I learned from him."

"Why did he retire?"

"Exhaustion I'd say."

"You mean from fighting?"

Colton laughed. "No, Mac is Irish—fighting never tires him. It invigorates him. No, it's the service itself. The army takes and takes and doesn't give much back. Whatever satisfaction you get out of it has to come from within yourself. You can feed on your own resources for only so long."

I struggled to understand that, but mother seemed to know what he meant.

"Did the death of his wife have anything to do with it?"

Colton cocked an eyebrow. My God, he was handsome when he did that.

"He told you about it?"

Mother hesitated. "No."

"Well, I think that was the final blow. I've seen Mac hurt physically many times—terrible wounds you can't imagine—but this was as if he had been struck by lightning."

"Please tell me about her."

"Margaret McGregor was the most regal lady in the Southwest—present company excepted. Even the youngest men in the regiment were in awe of her. And she treated each one as if he were her favorite son."

"Can you tell me how she passed?"

Colton set down his cup. "We had a regimental ball. In the early evening she said she wasn't feeling well and went to lie down. She never woke up. Mac found her. I came in right after. She was lying on the bed still in her ball gown. She just looked as if she were sleeping. But she was gone. She was forty-eight years old. The doc said it was probably a blood clot. I don't know. But I'll tell you, I'd have cut off my right arm at that moment if it could have restored her to life. But she had slipped away before we even had a chance to say goodbye. Like a delicate morning mist when the sun comes up. Gone."

Tears—for Mac, I'm sure—filled mother's eyes.

"Theirs was a great love affair," Colton said. "The kind you read about in books. One night about a month before she died, Mac and I were sharing a quiet whiskey. Mac seemed especially thoughtful that night. He said, 'Wade, Maggie and I have been married twenty-seven years, and when I hear her voice in the next room my heart still jumps.'" He shook his head. "A lesser man would have broken. But he had the regiment. The men she had loved as much as he did. So he stayed for them. He was tired, though. He knew it was time. When a replacement was found, the second of his two great loves ended. And he was right. It was time to go."

"But why?" mother said. "I don't understand."

He thought for a moment. "Do you know how when someone breaks a leg and it doesn't heal right and he walks with a limp forever after? That was Mac. After Margaret passed, Mac's spirit hobbled along with a limp. Only the men closest to him could see, but it was obvious to us."

Colton seemed as if he were about to say more, but he stopped in mid-breath.

Mother refilled his cup, and I just stared at him. Finally, he seemed to make up his mind.

"Until last night," he said. "The limp was gone."

"Why?" mother asked in a voice barely above a whisper.

"I can only guess."

"Please . . . ."

"I think it was because of the corporal here," he said, smiling at me. Then he looked meaningfully at mother. "And because of her commander."

The tears slid down mother's cheeks.

"I'm sorry," she said and got up from the table and hurried over to the wash basin and wiped her face.

"Of course, I could be wrong," Colton said. "It might just be

that he'd eaten particularly well at the fiesta."

Mother spun around, smiling through her tears. "You're terrible!"

"I know," he said with a grin, and he looked at me and winked.

"Are you married, captain?"

"Yes, Ma'am."

"God bless you both."

Mother finished wiping her face and came and sat back down.

"Can you tell us about Mac's service?"

"If I had a month. Too many campaigns, Ma'am. Too much to tell."

"Just some hints, then."

He hesitated, as though groping for something to sum it all up.

"How about this?" he said finally. "General Crook has been known to call him Red."

Crook! He was a legend out here. The greatest of all the Indian fighters. Relentless in battle but a champion of the Indians after he had subdued them.

"He knows Mac?" mother asked in amazement.

"They served together at least twice. After some of the early Apache campaigns, Mac served on the northern plains against the Sioux and Cheyenne. He rode with Crook at the Battle of the Rosebud. He was part of the notorious Starvation March, where the soldiers ran out of supplies and were reduced to slaughtering and eating some of their own horses. It took a terrible toll on the men. Mac told me once that he felt that his health was never the same after that ordeal. Though you'd never realize it to look at him now."

"Did he know Custer?" mother asked.

"Fleetingly I think. Not well at all. Custer isn't one of his favorite topics."

"Why?" I could not help asking.

Apacheria

"Well, corporal, in Mac's view any arrogant officer who leads his men to horrible deaths has a place reserved for him in Dante's Inferno."

That seemed to trouble mother. "That sounds very harsh."

"There are a couple of other reasons as well. The first is the way Custer drove his men. He hammered them. Custer was a magnificent physical specimen, and he assumed his men should be. He ground them down into dust. His punishments were harsh, too. And they hated him for it. He had no time for them as men, either. I doubt you could find a single person in the army who ever witnessed Custer speaking to an enlisted man. Even many of his officers detested him. Certainly Reno and Benteen did. Especially Benteen. And the troopers . . . to Custer they were just bodies in blue. Servants to his glory. And Mac loathed him for it."

"But surely some of his men must have liked him," mother said.

"A few did. Ironically one was a good friend of Mac. He was a fellow Irishman. Hailed from County Carlow. He died on the ridge above the Greasy Grass. He was the captain in command of Company I. Supposedly some of the troopers on that ridge killed their own horses to form breastworks, but he wouldn't kill his horse. He died on foot, firing back and still holding his horse. One of the Indians said that when they found him his fingers were still gripping the reins of his horse, who was standing there over him like a sentry despite multiple wounds. Don't know if that's true, but that's the story. He was one of the few men who wasn't mutilated afterward. Not while holding that horse in death. Bad medicine."

"Who was he?" mother asked.

"His name was Myles Keogh. He'd fought for the Pope in the Italian wars. His death hit Mac hard."

"Did the Indians take the horse?" I asked.

"No, they wouldn't touch him. The soldiers shipped him

back on the *Far West* and nursed him. He's living the good life at Fort Riley. No one is allowed to ride him ever again. His name is Comanche." Colton smiled. "I saw him once. Mac had some business at Fort Riley, and he ordered me and Sergeant Ryan to go with him."

Colton seemed wistful.

"Late in the afternoon, we went looking for Mac after he was done talking with the colonel. We couldn't find him anywhere. Suddenly Paddy Ryan burst out laughing. 'An Irishman has an eye for two things,' he said. 'Good whiskey and good horseflesh.' I followed Ryan to the stables. Sure enough, there was Mac with Comanche. They stood in the shade of an old tree near the stalls. Comanche has the complete run of the fort like a camp dog. They stable him only at night."

"What were they doing?" I asked.

"Mac had his right arm hooked around Comanche's neck, and with his other hand he was stroking him gently on the forehead. He was speaking to the old warhorse. I assumed he was confiding in him, the way a tough and lonely man will confide in a faithful dog. But now . . ."

He hesitated.

"What, captain?" mother said.

"Now I think it was the reverse. I think he was asking the horse to confide in *him*. To unburden himself of the horrors he had witnessed. To finally let go of the terrible secrets only Comanche knew."

I stared at the captain in wonder. Thoughts like those simply dazzled me.

"Ryan and I stood there in the sun for a long time. We'd have baked there for a week rather than interrupt. Finally Mac pressed a cheek against Comanche's face, said something I couldn't make out, and turned away and walked off slowly and alone."

Colton gazed at the back of his hands, but it was clear he was looking at something else. He seemed torn.

Finally, he said, "Ma'am, I'll share one thing more with you. Margaret told me this and I think I might be the only person other than her who ever knew it." He folded his hands in a relaxed fashion and looked up at mother. "The day he found out that Custer had died, Mac wept."

We both just stared at the captain in silence.

"And he came back here after the plains wars?" mother said at last.

"He prefers the warm weather. And he's Catholic, so he likes living among the Mexicans instead of the chilly Scandinavians up north. Most of all, though, he loves Apacheria."

"Can you tell us any more about his service down here, captain?" mother asked. "Some details maybe?"

"Even before the Rosebud, he had fought in this land. He was with Bourke and Jeffords when they met Cochise up in the Dragoon Mountains. He doesn't talk about it much, but when he's in the right mood he'll tell you that Cochise was the most extraordinary human being he ever met. Besides Crook, of course. Some of Mac's old comrades told me that when word came that the great warrior had died in his stronghold in the Dragoons—he must've been in his mid-sixties by then—Mac was not to be seen for the rest of the day. I know what he was doing. He was lifting a glass of Irish to the dead chief."

"Captain, I don't understand," I said, trying not to sound too stupid.

Colton smiled. "Katy, don't feel strange asking. I asked him, too. He said, 'Wade, when a great wolf falls, you weep. It doesn't matter that he tried to eat your young, you mourn his passing.' Mac knew that a world without Cochise would always be a lesser place. He said that the heroic figures were all passing away. He knew the West was changing, and I think he wondered if it was really for the better. Mac isn't just a soldier in the West, he and the old-timers *are* the West. He knows that when the West passes, he'll pass with it."

"Did Cochise just die a normal death?" I asked.

"Jeffords, one of his few white friends, said that cancer of the stomach struck him down. Did what no bullet could ever do. He's buried in a secret grave in the Dragoons."

"You soldiers are such strange men," mother said. "You battle the Apaches without quarter and then"—she shook her head—"I don't know."

"A cavalryman respects no man more than one who is worthy of his steel. None is worthier than the Apache."

"What about Manolete?" mother asked.

Colton's eyes grew wary. "What about him?"

"Mac told me they had met."

"Yes."

"How did that happen?"

"I can tell you nothing about that."

"Oh, I'm sorry. I didn't realize you didn't know about it."

"I do know about it."

"I don't understand."

"Ma'am, it's not important that you don't understand."

That seemed rude. Mother was clearly caught off guard by the captain's change in tone.

"I didn't mean to pry."

"Mac and Manolete is a private matter not to be discussed by me."

"Very well, but—."

"That's all there is to say. Ask Mac about it. Or if you have the terrible thrill of meeting Manolete someday, you can ask him. I can tell you nothing."

Mother got up and cleared away the dishes and said no more.

The silence was as heavy as a horse blanket.

She started clattering around the cups and plates at the washstand when Colton went over to her. She turned to face him.

"Ma'am, you know ranchers and farmers. You don't know soldiers. Not yet. Their battle experiences are in a secret safe

locked away. Few are allowed into that darkness. And then only rarely. My father fought at Cold Harbor in the War. He spoke to me about it maybe three times my whole life. Do you see what I mean?"

"Yes," she said softly.

"I think I've offended you. Please accept my apology. But I cannot open Mac's safe for you. If he chooses to do that someday, it will mean more than you'd ever have imagined. But don't pat yourself on the back too soon. It's a fearful charge to be allowed to gaze into a soldier's soul."

Mother stood there in silence. Then her eyes softened and the tiniest hint of a smile curled the corners of her mouth.

"Captain, don't take it amiss if I tell you that your wife is a very fortunate woman." A full smile flowed from her lips, and she held out her hand. "Wade, it's a very great privilege to know you."

6

For all his eagerness to return to the fort, Captain Colton found many reasons to linger. He loved to tell stories, and he entertained us with anecdotes about his fellow soldiers. It was close to noon before he was interrupted. The rumble of wagons brought mother and me to the front door.

"What on earth . . . ?" she said and hurried outside.

A pair of wagons creaked under the weight of hundreds of adobe bricks.

"*Buenos tardes*, Pino," mother said to one of the drivers. "What are you doing?"

"Delivering. Where do you want these?"

"You have the wrong place."

"There is only one Señora Malone. I'll be here with the workmen Monday morning to build the casita."

"Casita? What are you talking about? Who paid for this?"

"*El Coronel.*"

We heard Colton laughing on the porch behind us.

"That's Mac," he said. "Few words and much action."

Mother turned to Colton, but he shook his head.

"He can be a mystery, the colonel."

"Just stack them somewhere over there, Pino," mother said in exasperation.

She went back into the house and we followed.

Apacheria

"I'm not accustomed to someone taking charge of my life," she said, pacing back and forth in front of the kitchen window.

"He's a colonel in the army, Ma'am. Taking charge is his business."

"We'll see."

"May I offer an opinion?" Colton asked.

"By all means."

"He's having it built so he can stay there." Colton looked at me uncertainly and then said to mother, "He doesn't want to compromise your reputation by sleeping under the same roof."

"Oh, for heaven's sake, I don't care about that."

"He does."

"But the money. How can I—."

"Don't concern yourself with that. Mac can afford it. He's been very frugal. You have to understand that out here soldiers have only two things to spend their money on—whiskey and women. He's always been temperate with whiskey, and he's always been loyal to one woman. So he's accumulated some silver over the years."

"If he's building a casita, does that mean he's staying permanently?" I blurted out.

The hope in my voice was not lost on Colton.

"Corporal, one of the first lessons a soldier learns is that nothing in life is permanent except toil and God."

Mother looked at him thoughtfully. "That's very beautifully said, captain."

"My father was an eloquent man."

She smiled. "Will you stay the night?"

"Alas, my new colonel awaits. I should be on the trail." He reached for his hat. "I'd like to leave a note for Mac, and I'll head out."

"Then Godspeed. And thank you for sharing your time with us."

Mother was a hard taskmaster the rest of the day. It was clear that she wanted our home gleaming by evening. In the late

afternoon I managed to elude her. I wandered out to the little stream that flowed from our property down to the San Pedro. Winter rains had been good this year, so the cottonwoods along the banks looked wonderful. I found a shady spot under a big tree and sat by myself.

My emotions were driving me crazy. Too much had happened over the last day and a half. I was happy and nervous and afraid and overwhelmed. I felt like singing and yet was also sure that I could burst into tears at any moment. I did not know where to turn. I was certain that even mother would not understand.

She found me easily. I was relieved she did not scold me for shirking my chores. She sat beside me and handed me her canteen without saying anything. I took a sip and gave it back to her. She corked it and set it on the ground.

I guess I sighed one too many times. She reached over and put an arm around my shoulders. I just leaned against her.

"It's not easy being eleven," she said, staring out across the stream.

"Not without a daddy." I had no idea where that came from. It just tumbled out.

"I know." she said. "I'm sorry."

"Oh, no, I didn't mean it that way."

"That's all right, Scamp. A little girl needs a father. It's just that I never found anyone suitable."

"Then they shouldn't have been called suitors," I said with a smile.

She laughed and kissed me on the nose.

I stretched and gave her a peck on the cheek.

"I know this is a difficult time for you," she said. "You're feeling things . . . ."

I was embarrassed and looked away.

"Don't worry. Timmy is a good boy," she said.

My face felt like it had ignited.

Apacheria

"It's nothing to be ashamed of," she went on. "Those are normal feelings. Good ones. Necessary, too." She stroked my hair. "If I hadn't had them, you wouldn't be here."

What mother did not say, and what I would not realize until I had girls of my own, was that a girl needs a safe man nearby when she begins to flower. A man in whose eyes she can see her beauty and power reflected and admired without fear or danger. There was no man like that in my life. There never had been.

"Lord knows, I've looked," mother said, more to herself than to me. "Maybe I've looked too hard."

"You'll find someone. I know you will."

"Finding isn't the most important thing. Accepting is. Remember that always."

"Like Timmy?"

"Maybe. Only you'll know and that'll take time."

"But I don't understand boys. They don't make sense."

Mother smiled. "Do you know what question you'll ask yourself most often for the rest of your life?"

I shook my head no.

"How could God come up with creatures so strange? And, even better, why on earth would He want to?"

I giggled. "Do you know?"

"No one knows—except God. And He's not telling."

I laughed. "Then why don't we just ignore them?"

"We try. They're so blind and crude sometimes that we'd like to. But women and men are only half beings without the other. Never forget that. And always remember that as maddening as men are, life would be a very bleak journey without them."

"And they fight for you. Like Timmy did for me."

"A man will walk on broken glass for the woman he loves. Do it without a second thought. And when the snows come, he's the wall against the winter wind."

"I like that."

"So do I," she said wistfully and looked away. "For a

mature woman . . . for a woman with seasoning, only a man can build a lasting fire against the night."

I picked up some pebbles and began tossing them one at a time into the stream.

"What about Jim, mom?"

Now it was her turn to sigh. "If it were the right thing now, it would've been right years ago. It wasn't and it isn't."

"Then why—?"

"Because we've been playing a game. A stupid adult game. One that I never want you to play."

I did not know what she meant.

"I want you to be a more honest woman than I am, Scamp."

"Oh, mommy, no one could ever be. Not ever."

I think this day was the first time I realized how lonely she was. She had poured so much of herself into our lives, just so we could survive, that all other concerns had been pushed aside. But her needs now recoiled like the snap-back of a bullwhip—with speed and with pain.

"Time to get going," she said. "Mac might be at the house by now."

"I think I hear riders," I said, turning toward the river in the distance.

Mother strained to see. "From the south?"

"I think so."

"Let's get back."

She grabbed my hand and pulled me up a little too fast. I grunted.

"I'm sorry," she said. "But let's not dawdle here."

The sun was very low when we reached home. Mac had not gotten back yet. We went inside and mother bolted the door. She lit some lamps, and I realized why the house had seemed different yesterday after Mac had been here a while. He had moved most of the lamps very close to the windows, so it was impossible to walk between a lamp and the window and create a silhouette.

Apacheria

Mother took the shotgun from above the fireplace and got a box of shells from a kitchen drawer and loaded it.

The sound of the riders was growing louder.

Mother hurried to a front window. I was right behind her and we looked out together.

The last low rays of the sun caught the riders full in the face. They were white men.

"It's Scabby," I said.

I heard mother let out a long relaxing breath. "I never thought I'd be so happy to see him."

She set the shotgun against the wall near the door and stepped onto the porch. I went out beside her.

"Any luck?" mother asked.

"None today," Scabby said. "But we heard rumors that Manolete is on the move and making his way up the San Pedro." He pointed to the troughs. "Water for our horses?"

"Of course. And I have hay and grain if you need it."

Scabby seemed surprised by her hospitality. "Thank you, Mrs. Malone."

"You're welcome, Norbert," she said, using his real name.

While the horses were drinking, I heard hoofbeats off to the right. I turned and saw Mac riding in from the west.

"Mrs. Malone, why don't you come to town with us? You're not safe here."

She turned and smiled as she saw Mac ride up. "Oh, I think we're safe enough."

Scabby watched Mac approach. "Well, maybe you are."

"Hello, Scabby," Mac said as Reba brought him to the edge of the porch.

"Colonel."

"Any news?"

"He's on his way."

"Up the river?"

"That's what we're told. By the way, that was a nice little stunt you and the sheriff pulled — in the front door and out the

William Altimari

back."

"Oh, hell, we were just protecting you from yourselves."

The light was failing, but I was almost certain I saw Scabby smile.

"Well, maybe you were. Maybe you were."

"A piece of advice?" Mac said.

"Give it."

"Leave this to the army. He's tougher than you, Scabby. Tougher than all of you."

"We can't wait. The wheels of the army roll too slow."

"I won't argue with that."

Scabby turned to the men. "Ready?"

They nudged their mounts away from the troughs.

He raised a hand and off they rode.

"He isn't such a bad fellow really," Mac said, watching him go.

"He's Norbert Willoughby and comes from a good family," mother said. "He works at the feed store when he's not playing Custer."

"Let's hope he doesn't play him too accurately." Mac looked at me. "And how are you this evening, green eyes?"

"I'm very good."

Mother smiled and tousled my hair. "Hungry, Mac?" she asked.

"Like a Catholic coyote fasting for Lent."

She laughed. "I fried up some chicken this afternoon."

"Corporal, will you tend to Reba for me?"

"I will."

I treated Reba like a princess because I knew she was Mac's princess. Then I hurried back to the house. I was happy. Tonight we had our fire against the darkness.

Mother was getting the food ready and boiling a kettle of water. She often liked to serve tea in the evening.

Mac was placing a new hat on our little dining table. It was just like his old one, buff with about a four inch crown and a

three or four inch flat brim. It struck me as odd that he would get a new cavalry hat now.

"Come here, Katy," he said in the voice of a commanding officer.

I went over to the table.

Mother stopped what she was doing and folded her arms and gazed at me with that half-smile.

"It's time for a promotion," Mac said.

"Already?!"

"Yes, indeed. One of the things you have to learn about the army, Malone, is that no one ever really wants to *be* a corporal."

I stood as straight as I could.

"There's no greater honor than a field promotion," he said. "Step forward, Lieutenant Malone."

He took the hat and placed it on my head.

"I had to guess about the size. Looks like I guessed right."

My grin must have stretched from here to Tombstone.

"It needs a little character," he said and he took it over to the tea kettle. He held it above the steam for a bit to soften it and then pinched the crown and put it back on me.

"Very nice," mother said.

"Now to make it official," he said and reached for his own hat. He pulled off the twisted yellow cavalry cord from the crown and placed it around mine. It was faded and battered and had a hundred tales to tell.

"Oh, Mac," mother said, "not that."

"Don't be silly," he said.

"But it's been through so much."

"That's why it belongs on Katy. Most soldiers throw theirs away as just another of the army's useless annoyances. And it is. But I've always kept mine." He adjusted the twin fobs tied at the ends and laid them across the front of the brim. "There." He looked into my eyes and grinned. It was the greatest grin in the history of the world.

I threw my arms around him. The brim knocked against his

chest and pushed the hat to the back of my head.

"Thank you so much," I said, squeezing him hard.

I turned to mother. She looked happy and yet her eyes were misty. She could be deeply affected by the craziest things. She bit her lip and spun around and went back to preparing supper.

We had a simple meal and a perfect one. Mac had brought a bottle of Spanish wine, and that mellowed out mother very nicely. I had never seen her so relaxed. She even let me have a little bit. "In honor of your promotion," she said and handed me a small glass.

The coyotes began yipping. No matter how far away they were, they always seemed like they were just under the window. A while later our horned owl took up his place in one of the cottonwoods and sang to us with his single haunting note.

"Do you know an old rancher named Devlin?" Mac asked mother and poured her some more wine.

"Yes. Remember? It was his place where they caught the two Apaches stealing grain."

"Oh, that's right. He's selling out."

Mother frowned. "Are you sure?"

"He was at the bank while I was there. He wasn't shy about it."

"He was here in the old days. During the earlier Apaches wars."

"He's running scared now."

"I guess he has a long memory."

"For whatever reason, it's not good. That's how a panic starts. If it doesn't stop, before you realize it the landlord is the owl out there and the only settlers are those desert song-dogs."

"It's really that bad?"

Mac sipped his wine. "I've seen whole communities scatter during an Indian outbreak."

"We'll never leave, will we, Scamp?"

"Nope."

Mac winked at me. "I expect no less from the lieutenant and her commander."

Apacheria

"Speaking of soldiers," mother said, "Captain Colton spent most of the day here."

"Did he? Why?"

Her wine-dreamy eyes smiled at him. "Because you asked him to."

"You did?" I said.

"It wasn't difficult to convince him. But I guess I have to rattle my brain a little harder if I want to fool your mother."

"Thank you for asking him," mother said. "Now what about that casita?"

I was glad for the effect of the wine on mother. It had dulled her anger over seeing Pino and his friend drive up with a couple of wagonloads of bricks.

"I can't keep stealing Katy's bed forever."

"Yes you can! I don't mind."

"Mac, I can't afford it. And I can't accept it as a gift, either."

"A long-term loan then. And besides, you really need to hire a hand. If you give him a place to sleep and cook him these good meals, he'll work for very little. You'll be able to afford it."

"But then what about you?" I said. "Where will—."

Mother looked at me sharply and I shut up.

Mac seemed not to notice.

Mother stared down into her glass. "Katy and I have had to struggle for a long time. But God has blessed us in other ways. We've never complained to Him." She looked up. "And now all this. . . ."

"All what?" Mac said. "It's almost nothing."

"Oh, you infuriating man!" She glanced at the cavalry hat pushed to the back of my head and then looked at Mac. "Don't you see? It's everything."

He sighed and leaned back in his chair. "Then I have no idea what I'm going to do with this." He reached behind the bib of his shirt and pulled out what looked like a wad of tissue paper. "Any ideas, lieutenant?"

"I think you should give it to this lady," I said, and this time

I did the winking.

He handed it across to her.

Mother unfolded the paper and held up a large Spanish high comb exquisitely carved from tortoiseshell.

"Oh, Mac." She was biting her lip again. "I . . . . Why . . . ?"

"For your kindnesses."

"*My* kindnesses?"

"I think the tortoiseshell goes with the auburn hair, don't you, lieutenant?"

"Oh, yes."

She reached out and laid her right hand on top of his. "Thank you. But don't give us any more. I can't bear it."

For the first time, I saw Mac baffled. For that matter, so was I. What could be better than getting gifts from this generous man?

"I don't understand, Mary."

"I'm not used to all this giving. I don't know. . . ." She looked down and shook her head. "The wine is affecting me. I'm having a hard time thinking."

"Let me help." He reached out and poured her some more wine.

For a moment, she just gaped at him, and then she burst out laughing. It was an absolute choir of laughter, unrestrained, unguarded, and overwhelming. It was as startling to me as if I had a pet songbird for years and then one day it sang a song I never knew it had. I had never heard anything remotely like this laughter from mother—a torrent of joy that came crashing out from the center of her soul.

7

By the time supper was done, we were all exhausted. I longed for sleep, and with all that wine mother could not hold out either. Mac offered to clean up, and she let him.

No bad dreams for me this night. But sometime after midnight the coyotes woke me. I turned over and noticed light fanning in under the door.

"Mommy," I whispered.

She moaned and rolled away from me.

I shook her.

"Mmmmm?"

"There's a lamp lit in the parlor."

That took a moment, and then she pushed herself up on one elbow.

"Do you think something is wrong?" I asked.

She got up and grabbed her dressing gown. When she went to the door and cracked it, I was right behind.

A single lamp burned. Mac was sitting in the large wing chair my father had built before I was born. Mac had taken off his boots and propped up his feet on a footstool. He seemed very comfortable nestled into the blue brocade. Yet his expression was dark as he stared off into a land I could not see. A bottle of whiskey and a glass sat on the small side table to his right. The glass was empty and the cork was still in the bottle.

"Mac . . . ." mother said gently.

I expected him to be startled, but he was not.

"Yes?"

"May we join you?"

"Yes."

We went in and sat across from him on our small sofa.

"Why are you troubled?" mother asked.

I noticed a note unfolded on the table next to Mac. I assumed it was the one from Captain Colton.

"Not troubled, just thinking."

Mother looked at the bottle and then back at Mac.

"May I make you a cup of tea?"

"No, thank you."

We sat in silence for a spell.

"I'm not sure why people look forward to retirement," he said finally. "It brings on too much thinking. All of a sudden a whole throng of men appeared to me. They marched across my mind like a Roman legion. Silly, isn't it? Cavalrymen hate to march."

"Who are they?" mother asked.

"The men I served with." He stared ahead, not looking at her. "They're all gone. Some are retired, most are dead. I was thinking about them tonight." He laughed. "The way they looked at me when I first came out here. It didn't matter how much you'd fought in the War. This was different. Ask the men who were made wolf meat at the Little Bighorn. They learned the difference too late."

Mother got up and put the kettle on and came back to the sofa.

"I have to laugh at myself now. A pathetic shavetail who thought he knew how to fight because he'd battled Johnny Reb. Those old horse soldiers gave me a sort of bemused look I didn't understand. I understand it now. And it's because of them I'm still alive. They didn't put on kid gloves, that's for sure. I got banged around. I cursed them under my breath more times than I can count. But they had so much knowledge. More than that—

wisdom. Monty and Mario and Jim. Charlie and Ralph and John and Steve. It's because of them I'm here to be with you now."

"Then I honor them," mother said.

"Most had little education. Some had none. But braver men never sat a saddle. I admired them more than they ever knew. And I cared for them. I'm sure not a single one knew of the affection I had for all of them." He turned to mother. He looked so sad. "My God, Mary, I wish I'd told them."

"Oh, Mac, don't worry, they know. God will make sure they know."

His eyes softened. "That's such a sweet thing to say. Thank you for saying that."

He seemed so boyish at that instant. I never knew a grown man could look childlike. He glanced at me and then turned away, as though he were embarrassed. How could a man like that be uncomfortable in front of a little girl? It made no sense. At that moment, all I wanted was to go over there and comfort him, but I was afraid to.

"Some of them I'd known for years before they ever opened up to me. It took a lot for them to do it. But that's what made me wise. The War was just one giant engine of destruction. No chance to think. But out here it was different. Plenty of time for thinking. And learning."

The water was boiling. Mother went over and brewed us some tea. When she approached Mac with a cup, she pointed to the bottle and glass.

"May I?"

"Yes."

She moved them aside and set down his cup on the table.

Mac blew on his tea to cool it. Then he handed mother the note lying next to him.

I leaned over her arm and read:

Share it with them. They care about you.
They should know.

"It's because those fine men shared some of themselves with me that I became a better man than I ever could have been without them. So tonight I want to share a story with you. I don't think it'll make you better" — he smiled — "that's not possible. But it might make you wiser. In any case, it'll tell you something about me. I hope it doesn't shock you."

He propped his left elbow on the thick arm of the chair and leaned his head sideways against two raised fingers and his thumb. He was staring away from us when he began.

"It happened many years ago. I was on leave. A friend of mine contracted with a rancher to bring a string of horses from Tucson to Contention. His name was Von Rempfer, though I think the nobility angle was fake. Everyone called him Dutchy. He asked me to help him. I had the time, so I agreed. He hired an ex-army scout to go with us. He was a leathery veteran named Maloney. He'd seen his share of Apache raiding parties in his day. We'd gone about ten miles on a spring day when the world changed forever. We were riding in single file through an *abra* when Maloney stopped and scanned the outcrops. He said he didn't like the lay of the place and the sooner we got through the better. The word 'better' was just out of his mouth when an arrow shot right into the side of his head and blew him off his horse. Dutchy never even got off a shot before they were on us. They were Chiricahua Apaches. Their leader was a giant the Mexicans called Manolete for some reason, though his Indeh name was Nantaje. They pulled us from our mounts. They wanted the horses and guns and supplies in the little mule wagon we had. Sometimes the Apaches take prisoners and sometimes not. This time they didn't."

Mac paused and stared fiercely into the past. The only sound was the owl outside calling his melancholy note.

"Discretion wasn't a word Dutchy understood. Even though a pair of Apaches was holding him, he let loose a stream of curses at every one of them and all their ancestors. They didn't understand English, but it didn't matter. The translation was on

Apacheria

Dutchy's face. Manolete whipped out a hatchet and split Dutchy from his forehead to his chin. Then they tied me to a wagon wheel while Manolete hacked out Dutchy's heart. He watched me while he did it to see my reaction. He threw the bloody heart onto Dutchy's cracked chest. Then he had his men gather up everything they wanted. They stripped the bodies and they stripped me. When they were ready, Manolete set the wagon on fire. I was still tied to the wheel and he waited to see if I'd beg. But begging is useless with Apaches. Finally, he turned his pony and rode off with his men. He left me to burn."

Mother and I were frozen in place. Nothing could have moved us now.

"I'd hoped the bindings would burn before I did. But they'd tied me well with strips of horsehide. The Apaches are experts at torture. What they didn't know they picked up from the conquistadores, those masters of pain. The dry old wagon flashed into a huge torch. I was tearing my wrists apart trying to get loose." He rolled up a sleeve and pointed to a long hairless strip on his right forearm. "The flames were getting me here, too." He showed us a pale swath of skin behind his right ear. "I vaguely heard shots somewhere, and the Apaches came riding like hell back through the *abra*. As they rode by, Manolete shot an arrow into me and then they were gone. I was screaming by now. Through tears and sweat I could make out a blue mass coming up the pass. It was a troop from my regiment. They'd run into the Indians as they were riding out of the *abra*. There wasn't any water to put the fire out, so a young lieutenant rushed forward and cut me out of there, risking himself to do it. A handsome fellow named Wade Colton. He tried to pull the arrow out of my shoulder, but the shaft broke and the obsidian head stayed in. They took me back to Huachuca. The post surgeon nursed me back. He wasn't eager to dig around in my shoulder for the arrowhead. He was afraid of damaging some nerves and crippling my arm." Mac tapped his shoulder. "It's in there still. They call obsidian Apache Tears. I shed a few that

day."

I just stared at Mac and sipped my tea. I hardly realized it was cold now.

"After I recovered, I was obsessed with avenging Dutchy but I never came close. Manolete was gone, probably to Sonora. Believe me, there are few things worse than vengeance denied. But there was to be an incredible sequel. Five years after Dutchy had been split open like a slab of rotten beef, I was staying briefly in Tombstone. One morning I heard a commotion down in Fremont Street. I looked out and saw the sheriff pushing along Manolete in handcuffs. People were throwing rocks at him but he ignored the hits. I ran down to the jail right away. The sheriff was beating him with a broomstick. Manolete had been found stealing food from a ranch house a couple of miles out of town. The owner and his young wife had been cut to pieces."

"Where were all Manolete's men?" mother asked.

"The power of the Apaches had long since been broken. Manolete had fled the agency alone. And now I was going to be the world's happiest man when I watched Manolete kicking and snapping at the end of a rope."

"But why was the sheriff beating him?" mother asked.

"On general principles and because Manolete wouldn't tell the sheriff his name. The stupid lawman didn't know it's a great impoliteness to ask an Apache his name directly. It should be asked only through a third party. So I told the sheriff he'd captured 'The Infamous Manolete.'"

"Did they give him a trial?" mother asked.

"A masterpiece of frontier jurisprudence. Lasted twenty minutes and the jury deliberated about fifteen seconds. But it didn't matter to me. They were going to hang him the next day and I just hoped his neck didn't break and that he strangled slowly."

I could not imagine Mac saying something so horrible. I did not know what to think.

"I went to see Manolete that night. He'd aged some and he was leaner, but he was still a magnificent specimen of savage

Apacheria

manhood. And the son of a bitch was completely unbowed. He sat on his cot ramrod straight. His hair was past his shoulders, a red silk soldier's neckerchief around his head. No shirt, cotton trousers, and buckskin moccasins almost to his knees. He had no English at all but he was fluent in Spanish. He didn't recognize me at first. I asked him if I should scream and then he might remember. He nodded slowly. 'Yes, I remember you. The horses.'

'The German, damn you!' I yelled at him.

'Yes, the German, too.'

"His coolness was maddening. Then he folded his arms across his chest and said, 'You are a very tough Irishman. I do not think you need a broomstick to prove it.'

'They're going to hang you tomorrow. Did you understand the trial?'

'Of course they are going to kill me. White men always kill Indeh. It is what they do best.' Then he shrugged. '*A quién la importa!* I have killed twelve Americans and seventeen Mexicans, some of them women. I have killed three babies and raised four as my own. But those two people today I found as they were. I did not kill them.'

"Then he laughed in the sad way that only an Apache can, and lay down and went to sleep."

Mac paused and took a sip of tea and smoothed down his moustache.

"So at last Dutchy was being avenged. Yet Manolete was sleeping soundly and I wasn't. I lay in bed that night and stared at the ceiling. So what if he was being executed for a crime he didn't commit? He deserved to die" — Mac spun around at us — "didn't he?"

I jumped when Mac did that, and I spilled my tea.

"I was leaping up and down inside and laughing. And it made me sick. A person can definitely sin inside his own mind. My own nauseating pleasure in the anticipation of this man's death made me an accomplice in a judicial crime — and I couldn't

bear it."

Mac set down his cup. He seemed as focused now as a beam of light.

"I got up around midnight. I found a couple of flour sacks in the kitchen of the rooming house were I was staying and cut a pair of holes in one of them. Then I put it on, stole a horse, and watched the jail until the sheriff went out on his rounds. One thing I learned from the Indians is how to move about silently. The poor deputy was sitting reading a newspaper when I placed the muzzle of my revolver against the back of his neck. I thought he was going to wet himself."

Mother covered her mouth to stop from laughing.

"I dropped the other sack on his head and tied it around his neck with a string. Cut off someone's vision and it just numbs him. He sat as still as if he were nailed to the chair. Of course, Manolete recognized me even with the sack over my head. He knew I'd waited years to blow his heart out, but with a Colt pointed at his face he wasn't in a position to argue. I had him take the sack off the deputy long enough to gag him, and then handcuff him to the cell bars. Then we were off. It seemed like we rode forever, Manolete riding bareback. I finally pulled up as the sun was rising over a low mesa. A brilliant sheet of pink flame fanned out behind a thin wash of clouds. Manolete turned on his mount and looked at me. The right side of his face was bathed in pink, and I think I saw in his eyes a dawning awareness of what was about to happen. I pulled my new Winchester out of its scabbard.

'If you're going to die, you'll die for the right reason, not the wrong one.' Then I handed him the carbine. 'Adios, Nantaje!'

"I slapped his horse and I saw him smile for the first and only time, and then the horse thundered off into the dawn. In his right hand the Infamous Manolete held the carbine, and his left hand was buried deep in the horse's mane. His hair flew out behind him and he was on fire in the stunning pink light—an awesome and timeless being." Mac's eyes narrowed. "And I

hated him. I hate him still. And setting him free was the greatest thing I've ever done in my life."

Maybe it was the weariness or the wine, but mother seemed overwhelmed by Mac's story. She turned away and I hugged her.

"I've never met a man like you," she whispered so low that Mac could not hear, but I heard. "Oh God, please help me."

"And now," Mac said, "now I have to stop this same man from riding up the San Pedro and killing the two women who've taken me into their hearts."

I went over and slid next to Mac on the big wing chair and rested my head in the hollow of his shoulder. I could feel a bump under the side of my face. Possibly it was a lump of scar tissue that had formed about the arrowhead. He wrapped an arm around me. Out in the cottonwoods the owl had stopped, but the coyotes had begun again their mournful wail.

8

Mass always bored me. It was not church that was the problem. Church was fine, and being there was always pleasant to me. The smell of beeswax and old wood and the lingering hint of incense comforted me in a way like no other. Mass, though, made me drift. I spoke to Jesus every night in my room, and I enjoyed that, but I could not keep my mind from wandering during Mass. This Sunday, though, was special because Mac came with us. Our little adobe church was not as crowded as usual. Many of the regular churchgoers were probably still sleeping off the effects of the fiesta. Of course, the Mexican women were there. They would always be there. And the Mexican men were where they always were, not inside church but outside smoking cigarettes and gabbing while their wives prayed for the salvation of their souls. What an odd custom. Here we were at church in the Arizona Territory with a Mexican priest, and most of the men inside were Irish or German or Italian.

    Mac disappeared shortly before Mass. When I asked mother about it, she pointed to the confessional at the side of the church, near the statue of Our Lady and the array of red votive lamps lit by the faithful.

    Mother silently prayed her rosary while we sat in the pew and waited for Mass to start. When Mac came back from Confession, he seemed happy and refreshed.

Apacheria

I tried to pay attention during Mass, but it was hopeless. I prayed that Our Lord would understand. My mind was all over the map. A few days earlier, I was just a little girl in a small town in the great expanse of the American Southwest. Now I felt I was on the edge of some great adventure. Because of a thirsty horse and a sneeze and a smile, my world was spinning wildly toward some unknown purpose. And I knew that those events had not been chance. Mother had taught me that coincidences were not that at all. She said that they were simply God's way of remaining anonymous.

One thing I hated about Mass was Clete Lomaddis. Every week he sat in the last pew and stared at the ladies as they came to church in their Sunday finery. I was convinced he was there just to leer at them. But Padre Tomas would never throw him out. He was always an optimist. Which a priest should be, I think.

When we left church, Mac made sure I was between him and mother as we walked down the street. I think he did that so people would not assume he and mother were a couple. From his point of view, that made sense. He must have known that there were many eligible men in town who would have fallen over themselves at an opportunity to court mother. He would not want to limit her chances. Mother, however, had a different view. When Mac maneuvered me between them, I saw by the look on her face that it was not to her liking. She would have been even angrier if she had realized I was smiling on the inside. It was fun for me to see her not always get her way.

The Paradise was the only place open for dining on Sunday. Mac insisted on treating us, and we got our usual table. The meal was good as always, and we had fun in each other's company. Then Lomaddis and some of his friends showed up and took a table close by. They were loud, deliberately so, I'm sure. I saw mother clench her jaw. Mac noticed it, too. The words "Shapiro" and "Jew" were being thrown about as if they were curses or slurs.

"Keep it down," Mac said.

Lomaddis turned. "Are we disturbing the ladies?" he asked in a silky tone.

"You're disturbing me."

"Our apologies."

Every time I saw him I wished I were a man so I could pound him into the ground. But that would also have meant another trip to Confession.

"What does he do for a living?" Mac asked mother.

"The rumor is he steals stock and sells it in Sonora," she said. "He claims he inherited money, but no one believes that. He's from some horrible place in New York. I forget the name."

"It's called The Devil's Dining Room," I said.

Mac laughed. "Hell's Kitchen."

Mother nodded. "That's it."

"Has he ever broken rocks?"

Mother gave him a puzzled look.

"Done time."

"I don't believe so."

"Mrs. Malone!" Lomaddis shouted.

Mother turned her head to look a him, but she did it slowly, as if it were an effort.

"Yes?"

"We're going to be neighbors. I bought old man Devlin's place. Bought it for a handful of beeeeeeads. Like Manhattan."

"How very nice for you. Just be careful not to cross the fence line. I have a shotgun with a faulty trigger. I've been known to shoot people. Accidentally, of course."

Lomaddis could smile and sneer simultaneously. It was truly a sight. He was angry at being belittled in front of his friends.

I looked at Mac. He was enjoying listening to mother as if she were an actress reciting Shakespeare.

Lomaddis was struggling with his smile, but it was twisting into a grimace.

Laughter from a few of his friends made his glare at mother all the more frightening. But she just turned away with contempt.

"Are we done?" mother said to the both of us.

"I believe we are," Mac answered.

We left the hotel. On the boardwalk a few feet from the door, Timmy was shining boots for pennies. He saw us and waved at me. I smiled and waved back.

"Excuse me a moment," Mac said and went over and chatted with him.

"Timmy never rests," mother said with a mixture of admiration and concern.

Mac rejoined us and asked what we wanted to do for the day. Mother believed that the Sabbath was precisely that, a day of rest divinely ordained. She kept it when she could and made sure I did the same.

"Katy and I would like to do absolutely nothing."

Mac smiled. "I could get comfortable with this retirement business."

That I doubted. It was clear that he was accustomed to being busy. I assumed the army believed Padre Tomas's dictum that an idle mind was the Devil's workshop. Even when Mac was relaxed, as he was now while he scanned the street, he was alert. He missed nothing. If we were walking down the street and a stranger were slinking along a wall fifty yards away, Mac would see him, assess any possible threat, and move on. I could not decide if this tireless watching were the result of training or if it were a part of him. Certainly I had known other soldiers. I could not remember having seen this trait before, at least to the same degree. I had always considered cavalrymen formidable because of their physical strength and familiarity with weapons and, most of all, their mastery of the horse. But those were acquirable skills, and what I observed in Mac raced far beyond that. His consummate awareness of his surroundings and, even more, his unsparing realization of his place within those surroundings,

created an impression of such confidence that those who were near him felt serene and secure. Whether he felt that or not, I could not say, but even without thinking about it he engendered those feelings in others. A few years earlier, a couple of Pinkerton agents had come through town on the trail of some outlaws. One of the agents liked to flirt with mother. I learned from him that the motto of their agency was "We Never Sleep." That came back to me now. I could sleep because Mac did not, not fully, ever. He was always there, on patrol for me and mother. I felt a little bit guilty about that, about the toll it must take on him. And yet his presence, like a great castle wall, brought me such comfort and peace that I could not imagine how I could ever live again without it.

Sheriff Blaine came out of his office across the street. He was dressed in a steel-gray suit and white shirt with a high starched collar. He was sporting a derby, a rare look for him. Even on Sundays he made his rounds. He had no deputy or other helpers, so people expected him to. He obliged because he was a dedicated servant to them. And also because his social life was very lean, to say the least. He was the sort of man almost no one disliked but whom few — other than mother — warmed to. A casual game of cards or a beer with a few acquaintances at one of the quieter saloons seemed to answer his social needs.

"Good morning to you all," he said as he crossed the street.

There was a look of resignation in his eyes that I found sad and endearing at the same time.

"Have you come for the meeting?" he asked.

"No," mother said. "We weren't aware of one."

"It's about the Apaches."

"I don't understand why everyone is all in a flutter," she said. "Do they expect Manolete to come riding through town during breakfast?"

"You know how people are. You should be there anyway."

Jim was not exaggerating. Mother was one of the few women in town — perhaps the only one — expected by men to participate in every important civic venture. Though she was

only a store owner who led a quiet life with her young daughter, her moral stature among the townspeople demanded more. Her views were sought, and her opinion of someone's character carried more force than the approval of the Pope. It had always been that way. I remember even when I was very young hearing people say, "Did you ask Mary's opinion?" or "What did Mary think about that?" Sometimes people would come into our mercantile with unruly children. All a parent had to say was, "Don't disappoint Mrs. Malone," and instantly quiet reigned.

"Where are they meeting?" mother asked.

"The shaded area behind the schoolhouse."

"Would you mind, Mac?"

"Not at all. Katy and I will take a walk."

"No, no, you should come with us."

"Mary is right, colonel," Jim said. "Your views will be valuable."

I admired him for saying that, because I suspected he did not want to.

"Lead the way, sheriff."

It was cool and pleasant under the trees behind the school. The undertaker, Mr. Coombes—all of us children called him Mr. Tombs—had provided chairs and a few tables. Waiters from the hotel were setting down trays of lemonade.

The small group was a fair representation of the men of the town. Mr. Shapiro was there, and I ran over and gave him a hug. Some tradesmen and ranchers came, as did Padre Tomas. Even a traveling salesman who passed through a few times a year. Not many of these drummers made it to our little town. This one was the least dishonest of a bad lot.

Clete Lomaddis sauntered in, but I was more worried about the man with him.

"Mother," I whispered and touched her sleeve.

He was Alejandro Skeels, the most frightening man I had ever known.

"I see him," mother said.

She turned to Mac, but Mac had already spotted him.

Skeels was big for a half-Mexican. Bitter right down to the pit, he took in the world with blank buzzard's eyes. The rumor was that he was an illegitimate orphan who never knew his father and whose mother died young. Crime lurked in every crease of his face. He had ridden with Lomaddis, but he had vanished for about a year. Some said Chihuahua, others Texas. But now he was back, and that could be nothing but bad. That stare — the dead-eyed gaze of a scavenger — swept the crowd, and when a scavenger stares, something is about to die.

"Let's keep it informal," Jim said, stepping up before the group. "Most of all, let's keep it calm. Padre, would you care to offer a prayer?"

"I would," Padre Tomas said and hurried forward with tiny steps, as chubby men do.

He removed his hat and bowed his head. "Father in Heaven, Your hand is upon us to protect us. We ask Your guidance here. We implore the Holy Ghost to grant us the wisdom to know that all men — white and red — stand equal before Your throne. We ask this through Christ Our Lord."

"Amen," many in the crowd said, but I heard some snickering, too.

The padre went back to his chair, and I got him a glass of lemonade. He smiled and caressed my cheek as he always did.

"I don't know why we're even meeting," Lomaddis said before Jim could speak. "We find the Indians and kill them. Torch them all."

"*La infamia!*" Padre Tomas said.

"Unless you're a federal officer," Jim said, "how do you plan to do that? Without getting hanged, I mean?"

"There's only one law here," Lomaddis said. "Self-preservation."

Scabby was just arriving. He drifted toward Lomaddis and Skeels. I looked at mother. There was disappointment in her eyes. Scabby and Clete had been friends of sorts over the years. I think Scabby felt tougher around him, and Clete used him and

Apacheria

pumped him up and made him believe he was more formidable than he could ever really be.

"No one has been injured yet, let alone killed," Jim said. "Not even in Mexico, where the Apaches believe they have permanent killing rights."

"Shall we wait for a killing?" Mr. Devlin asked. "Is that what you want, sheriff?"

"It's my understanding you're not waiting at all. You're going to California."

"That's right."

"Then why are you here this morning?"

Mr. Devlin's face reddened, but he said nothing.

"Be reasonable, Jim," one of the ranch foremen said. "We're afraid. Afraid for our families."

"I know that, Ben, but panic never won a battle. We're townsmen or farmers or ranchers. We can't go blundering out there against a people who perfected raiding and killing hundreds of years before we were born. The army is here to deal with this. They're out there right now on patrol. Up and down the San Pedro looking for sign."

Jim had no way of knowing that, but I figured a little lie right now was at most a venial sin.

"May I say something, Jim?" mother asked.

I always got a flutter in my chest when mother was about to speak. This was when I was most proud to be her daughter.

"Yes, Mary. Please do."

She stood up and looked around at the crowd. "We have a gentleman here today with more experience in these matters than we have. More than all of us combined, in fact." She turned to Mac. "Colonel, can you give us a few insights?"

Mac seemed caught off guard. "Mrs. Malone flatters me. In any case, I'm not a member of this community. I have no right to speak here today."

"You have a duty to speak!" the padre said, jumping from his chair. "Speak, *coronel*, before people lose their minds and

their souls."

Mac's eyes smiled at him. Our pudgy little priest would not have squashed an ant, but he was as morally brave as any man in town. I was beginning to learn it was that kind of bravery Mac admired most.

Mac stood up and took his chair and glass of lemonade and went to the head of the semicircle of people. He set the chair beside him and put the glass on the seat and his hat next to it.

"You don't avoid a wolf simply by knowing what he eats. You do it by knowing how he thinks." His eyes scanned the crowd. "Am I unfair if I say that few of you know how Apaches think? And that not one of you knows how this particular Apache thinks?"

No one answered.

"Then you'd better start thinking now. You'd—."

"Think about what?" Skeels said in a heavy voice that always seemed to me had just oozed up out of the mud.

"About how not to die," Mac said. "You can't outride them. And I can promise you that you can't outfight them. So you'd better try to outthink them. Though from what I've seen so far this morning, that looks like a thin hope."

"Please, *coronel*, tell us what you believe we should do," Padre Tomas said.

"Right now, nothing. As far as we know, Manolete and his men are still in Sonora. They might stay there."

"And if they don't?" Jim asked.

"Then we'd better find out the reason they bolted. It might be nothing. It could just be they got drunk on tiswin and fled the agency. Or swilled some of that coffin varnish the good Christians call whiskey and sell them so they can enjoy the spectacle of Apaches making fools of themselves. On the other hand, I've never known Manolete to indulge so much that—."

"You know him?" Jim asked in surprise.

"Yes."

"Are you an Indian lover?" Skeels said.

"I'm an Indian killer. Do you want a tally?"

Skeels said nothing.

"Vhat does he vant?" Mr. Shapiro asked.

"He probably doesn't know that himself. More than likely he just wanted out. But I tell you if you enrage this man, there's going to be death rolling up and down this valley."

"Wouldn't he be better off staying on the reservation?" one of the farmers asked. "Where it's safe?"

"Have you ever been there?" Mac said.

"No."

"I have. Of course, they had a different reservation once. A magnificent one—the Dragoons. I helped put them there. And when General Howard made peace with Cochise in '72, he promised him and his people that place for eternity. Then a few years later, a handful of Indians left it and committed some crimes. So the politicians used it as an excuse to round all of them up and move them off. Be cheaper and easier, they said, to keep an eye on them if all the Apaches were in one place. And what did it matter? Cochise was dead, so there was nothing to fear from him. Eternity had lasted two years."

"Who cares now?" Lomaddis said. "That's ancient history."

"Is it?" Mac said. "Ask Manolete—if you dare. To him, it happened five minutes ago." Mac paused and took a sip of lemonade. I could see he was losing patience. "Imagine this. One of you commits a crime." He stared at Lomaddis. "Didn't you walk off with one of that gentleman's rifles without paying? If so, the sheriff will want to speak with you after the meeting." He looked around the crowd. "Imagine because of that act by this fool that the regiment from Huachuca shows up here tomorrow and moves you out. All of you. No negotiation, no compensation, no argument. They herd you off to a stinking, malaria-ridden sump called San Carlos. You'd think yourselves violated. Cheated and robbed. Embarrassed in front of your women, shamed before your children. Hard to believe that any man would want to kill because of that." He glared at them all. "Isn't it?"

William Altimari

The silence of the graveyard hung over the crowd. Only a cool breeze passing through the trees and the chirping of birds broke the stillness.

"But what do we do now?" Jim finally said. "We can't rewrite the past."

"We can make sure we don't repeat it. Don't make any promises to the Indians that the politicians won't let you keep. And no armed bands roving the countryside looking for Apaches they'll never find. No —."

"How do you know we'll never find them?" Skeels said, stepping up close to Mac.

"If you don't know the answer to that, you're even more stupid than you look."

I was suddenly afraid for Mac. He was unarmed, but Skeels had a skinning knife at his hip and he looked eager to use it.

"Skeels, stand aside," Jim said. "Explain what you mean colonel."

"You can't find Apaches without using Apache scouts, the way Crook does. Unless my eyes are failing, there aren't any Chiricahuas around town who are going to run down Manolete for you."

"We can follow sign as well as Apaches can," Jim said.

"No one can follow sign as well as Apaches." Mac turned to Skeels. "And if someone as rank as you is going after him, you'd better stay downwind. Otherwise Manolete will smell you a mile off."

I heard mother move beside me, and I looked up at her. She had a hand in front of her mouth to conceal a smile.

"The biggest mistake anybody can make you've already made at Devlin's place," Mac said. "You dragged in those two Apache boys. Pray Manolete never hears about that. It was an act without point and without honor."

Scabby laughed, but it was a forced and nervous laugh. "What does honor have to do with Apaches?"

Mac looked at Jim. "It's hopeless, sheriff."

"Please go on, *coronel*," the padre said.

Apacheria

Mac sighed and rubbed his eyes. "Unless you understand the importance of honor to the Apache, you'll never understand Manolete. I'm not talking about the honor of the Knights of the Round Table. Or some idiot Philadelphia Quaker talking about the Noble Savage. I mean the honor of a warrior race that values the humiliation and torture and destruction of its enemies as much as anything on earth. Manolete is ruthless beyond comprehension, and yet his piss is more honorable than half the people I've known in Arizona. Every dealing he's had with whites has involved treachery—always theirs, never his."

"But *we* didn't betray him," one of the ranchers said.

"To Manolete, the past is the present. It's an unbroken line." Mac looked suddenly tired, and he seemed to be groping for something they would understand. "Consider this. Back in Philadelphia, where I'm from, there are old colonial cemeteries. Some are totally forgotten now. Covered with weeds and dead leaves. Walk by one sometime and see how sad that feels. Up in the Dragoons, Cochise is buried deep in a secret gorge in his stronghold with his favorite horse and his favorite dog. The great chief knew he was dying and he wanted to spend eternity in the midst of his people. Now everyone is gone. But Cochise is still there, and he's all alone." Mac's eyes glided across the crowd. "Maybe God can forgive that sort of betrayal. Manolete won't."

Jim looked exasperated. "Your recommendation then?"

"Be wary and defensive, but let the army do its job. Stop playing soldier. Stand down from this fight and let this wind pass—and just possibly Manolete will pass you, too. If you don't, then fear for your lives and the lives of your children." Mac picked up his hat from the seat. "And God help you all."

He stepped away from the chair and walked straight at Skeels, who was blocking his path. At the last instant, Skeels gave ground and Mac brushed by him.

The look of hatred on Skeels' face was horrible.

Mr. Shapiro jumped from his chair and hurried up to Mac

and grabbed his hand. Mac shook hands and gave him a weary smile but kept moving.

"I've had enough, Mary," he said in a low voice and he walked by us and away.

9

Mac was quiet the rest of the day. He spoke about this and that on the way home, but his attention always waned. In the afternoon, he took out Reba and went riding alone.

Mother tried to read and then putter in the garden and later do some sewing, but she was unable to keep at one thing.

Mac returned before dusk, and he seemed lighter in spirit. I was starting to realize that Reba was a magic elixir for him, and he for her as well. They communicated with each other so subtly and intimately that I could not imagine that they could ever have existed separately from one another. He was her king and she was his queen. Together they fused into one extraordinary being. By this time of year, she had lost her winter coat. When she moved, every muscle rippled clearly beneath her coppery sheen. As Mac rode her, he spoke to her in an intuitive language only the most astute horse person could see or sense. It was pleasant to watch him groom her lovingly and feed and water her in the evening.

After a light supper, mother lit some lamps, and she and Mac and I sat in the parlor and chatted about little things. I suspect mother was worried that Mac might drift off again later into that dark land of the night before. So she kept him occupied. From the occasional smile in his eyes, I think he knew what she was doing and he enjoyed letting her. The odd thing was that mother did not see that, but I did. To me, she was the most

perceptive person alive. Yet that evening I began to learn that I was more sensitive to Mac's emotions than she was. It was similar to the way a daughter has a special relationship with her father that is unique in all the world. But as soon as I thought that, I pushed it out of my head. I had no right to think it. How could I expect a father's emotions from Mac? He barely knew me. I was just a little girl he had spotted sitting on a hitching rail.

"Can you tell us about General Crook and General Howard?" mother asked him.

He slid the footstool in front of the wing chair and propped up his feet.

"Both extraordinary men," he said. "But very different—opposites, in fact. Howard lost his right arm in the War. I forget which battle. And he won the Medal of Honor at Gettysburg. He's a very devout man. Congregationalist, I think. His religion has a lot to do with why he wants to give a fair deal to the Indians. He took just a few men with him in '72 and sought out Cochise in the Dragoons for a parley. It was an amazing act of bravery. Of course, he had Tom Jeffords with him and that helped. He—."

"Captain Colton mentioned Jeffords," mother said, "but he didn't tell us who he was."

"One of Cochise's few white friends. He'd been a mail superintendent out here just after the War. So many of his men were being killed by Apaches that he just got up one day and rode straight into the Dragoons to meet the man that everyone feared. He wanted to try to make a deal. Cochise was stunned by that act of courage, and they became fast friends. So Howard took Jeffords with him when he made peace in '72. That deal was a great feat, believe me. Not everybody likes Howard, though. Some of the soldiers and settlers out here think he's a sanctimonious hypocrite. I don't know him very well, certainly not as well as Crook. Yet I can tell you he's no hypocrite. He's a good and honest man."

"And successful, too, then?" mother said.

Apacheria

"Very much so. His biggest failing is the highhandedness that always comes with moral certainty. He can be patronizing to the Indians, too. Looking at the Apaches simply as Christ's lost lambs isn't helpful. But he means well and he does well. More often than not anyway. He's now the commander of the Military Department of the Platte."

I glanced at mother. She was loving this. Mac was a living chronicle of Arizona.

"How about if I make us some tea?" she asked.

He smiled and nodded.

She went to the stove and put water in the kettle.

"Thanks for staying with us," I said to Mac. I was not sure why I said that at that moment. It just came out.

He smiled and said, "Where on earth would I rather stay than here?"

I went over and slid next to him on the big chair. I rested my head as I had before in the hollow of his shoulder.

"Don't be sad," I whispered.

"Sad?" he said softly. "Why would I be sad?"

"About Mrs. McGregor."

"Ah, Captain Colton has been talkative."

"I'm sorry," I said quickly. "I shouldn't have said that."

He put his arm around me and cupped my shoulder. "Can I tell you a secret?"

"Yes."

"Right now, Margaret is gazing down and smiling a smile so beautiful it's lighting up the streets of Heaven."

I looked up at him.

"And do you know why?" he said.

I shook my head no.

"Because of a girl named Katy sitting right where she is at this moment."

I felt my lower lip begin to quiver, and I strained mightily to control it.

"And anyway," he said, "I should be thanking you."

I pushed up in surprise and stared into those aqua eyes. "Why?"

"For brightening this old soldier's twilight years."

"You're not old, Mac."

"Oh, Katy, I'm as old as Babylon's walls."

"What are you two plotting?" mother said as she came in with the tray. "Looks like a conspiracy to me."

"Katy and I were exploring the nature of human gratitude."

"Indeed," she said, smiling at me with her eyes. "My little girl is a precocious one."

I went over and mother handed me a cup of tea that I gave to Mac and then I took my own.

"You were going to tell us about General Crook," mother said, sitting back down on the sofa. "Katy, sit here while Mac has his tea."

"Crook is a difficult man to summarize," Mac said. "He graduated near the bottom of his class at the Point, and yet he's one of the finest generals in the army. He had a superb record in the War, like Howard. Later, after the Apache campaign, he was promoted above many other older officers. It caused plenty of envy and resentment. Some of that still lingers."

"Colton said you know him well. How did that happen?"

"Captain John Bourke. He's Crook's top aide and one of the finest officers who ever drew breath. He asked me to go with him on a mission for Crook. This was in '73. A year earlier, Cochise had made his separate peace with Howard, even though Crook was commander of the Department of Arizona at the time. Cochise wasn't bound by any of the agreements that bound the other tribes, and Crook resented it. And he had no say on Cochise's reservation in the Dragoons. Jeffords was the agent and he ran it with a free hand. Meanwhile some of the Indians from Cochise's band were still riding down and raiding in Mexico. Crook was fed up."

"None of this kind of thing makes it into the papers here."

"It might if journalists weren't liars or fools. Don't ever expect the truth in a newspaper."

Apacheria

"So what happened?"

"I went with Bourke and a few others to see Cochise. Bourke was just a lieutenant then, and so was I. Jeffords came with us as the intermediary. It turns out that it was a model reservation, other than the Mexican raiding. Jeffords didn't care about that. He hates the Mexicans because of what they've done to the Apaches over the years. Anyway, when we reported to the general, he backed off—a rare thing for him. He let the Chiricahua reservation stand."

"What about later, Mac?" I asked. "Captain Colton talked about the Sioux."

"Up on the Rosebud. That was a brutal fight. We fought for about six hours. Crazy Horse pounded us to a standstill. We lost almost as many men as he did, although the tally wasn't really high on either side. Crook claimed victory because at the end of the day we controlled the field, and the Sioux rode off. Crook had a point. Warfare isn't about killing, it's about control. But the Rosebud was a hollow victory. After the mauling we'd gotten, we were almost out of ammunition, and Crook didn't dare try to link up with our other forces like he planned. He had no idea how many Sioux might be out ahead of us waiting to pounce. One of the regiments we were supposed to meet was Custer's Seventh. We never got there and he was wiped out at the Greasy Grass."

"Did anyone blame Crook?" mother asked.

"Some did. But it was nonsense. Crook wasn't responsible for that catastrophe. Custer destroyed Custer."

"What about him?" she said. "We've heard so many stories over the years."

"I'm not the one to ask."

That was the first time I heard him be short with mother.

"I'm sorry," she said and glanced down at her tea.

Mac looked guilty. "No, I'm sorry. It's just that—."

"You don't want to say something bad about another officer, right Mac?" I said.

He smiled. "Katy *is* precocious, isn't she?"

Mother looked up. "You don't have to say anything about him. It's all right."

"What does it matter now?" he answered with a shrug. "He's long gone. But I'll say this. He was one of the bravest men who ever lived. But it was a bravery that was off the edge. Almost unhinged. The problem was that even his bravery was tainted. It stemmed mostly from his contempt for his enemies. There's no valor in making war against people you believe are fools or worse. To him, it was a hunt and the rebs and the Indians were game."

"You knew him then?" mother said.

"Not well. The sad thing was that he was really only a small boy's idea of a cavalry officer. His knowledge of tactics was meager, especially for someone who saw so much fighting in the War. His greatest flaw was that he labored under the delusion that he was an Indian fighter, instead of what he was, a mounted fool. He thought he was still fighting in the War. But Crazy Horse wasn't Johnny Reb. Custer learned that on a horrible afternoon in June."

"He was very dashing, wasn't he?" mother said.

"Oh, yes. The flowing curls, the buckskins. But the way he always surrounded himself with reporters and photographers soured my stomach. Someone told me that he was the most photographed officer in the army. I don't doubt it."

"How did his men feel about him?" mother asked.

"Love or hate. Nothing lukewarm." Mac looked thoughtful and seemed like he was about to say something and stopped. Finally, he said, "I'll tell you one last thing. I have no proof it's true, no evidence at all—other than a half-century of life on this earth. There are some who adore Custer's memory, absolutely worship at his shrine. But I believe that the wisest of them, when they're alone in the darkest watches of the night, believe that there was about Custer—though they'd never say it out loud—something ultimately ridiculous."

Apacheria

"And Crook?" mother said, steering the conversation back to something more pleasing to him.

Mac laughed. "You'd never know he was a general. He did know how to cultivate reporters, but there were no poses or histrionics."

"Is he fatherly then?" mother asked.

"Crook? God no. He isn't the coziest man you've ever met. And he's a miser with praise. Doesn't reward his staff half as much as he should. Bourke especially. I know that John has been hurt over the years by what looks like Crook's indifference. But that's just Crook. You can't take it personally. He's very reserved, even taciturn. Personal warmth has never been his long suit."

"And no fancy clothes and photographers?" mother said.

"He should stay away from the lens. He's as stiff as a rail. And the way he dresses — Lord, help us. In the field, he often wears a canvas hunter's jacket and a grotesque cork helmet. And he rides a mule, for God's sake. He looks like a prospector who lost his map. But he's the scourge of the Apaches. And they know it."

"He's here again, isn't he?"

"He's back as head of the Department of Arizona. No other white man who ever lived understood the Apaches the way he does. In that respect, Howard is hopeless compared to him. The same with the Eastern do-gooders who romanticize the Indians. Noble Savage and other assorted idiocies. Those people are as absurd as French philosophers."

"But not Crook . . . ."

"Silliness like that could never take root in that man. When he's in the field, he wages war against the Apaches without mercy. As they do against him. And after he crushes them, he's their greatest defender and champion. No general dares speak up for the Apaches the way Crook does. I'll tell you, Mary, I've been all over this West and seen every type of human spawned. Crook is the greatest man I've ever known."

Mother smiled. "Thanks for sharing all this. You should write your memoirs someday."

He laughed. "Nobody wants to read the ramblings of a broken down old horse soldier. Besides, history is for the younger generation to compile." He looked at me. "So pay attention, Katy. You could be the one."

That stunned me. I turned to mother.

"Well, Miss Hentz says you do have a way with words. Why don't you start a diary?"

"Do you think I could?"

"Certainly. You can begin with last Friday."

Of course that's when I'd begin! That was when Mac rode in.

"Why Friday?" he asked, looking puzzled.

Mother turned away and gathered the cups. "No reason." She picked up the tray. "Time for bed, Katy."

How could I sleep now? The thought of the diary excited me so much. I was about to argue with mother about going to bed, and then Mac said, "Good night, lieutenant."

It sounded like an order.

"Good night," I said to both of them and trudged off to bed.

I undressed without bothering to light a lamp and I put on my nightdress. But I just lay there and stared upward in the darkness. Mother and Mac continued speaking in low tones in the parlor.

Then I did something I knew I should not have done. I slipped out of bed and tip-toed across the room. The creaking floorboards sounded like shrieks to me. I sat by the door and was surprised to hear they were speaking about me.

"She's a good girl," mother was saying. "She's a handful, though."

"She has a lively mind."

"Oh, yes. She exhausts me sometimes. But she's the beat of my heart."

A long silence followed, and then Mac said, "She's hooked me, Mary."

Apacheria

"I know."

"I can't get away."

"Do you want to?"

A pause, and then, "When she smiled at me from that rail, my whole world changed. It felt like it had spun off its axis. I can't explain it. Good God, I can barely describe it. And then when she took my hand and led me into the store . . . ."

It sounded as if he wanted help finishing what he was saying, but mother gave him none.

"When I turned around and was about to leave the store, I felt awful. What made you call me back?"

"God works in strange ways."

"What way?"

"The look on Katy's face when you were about to go."

I heard the clink of Mac's teacup as he set it down. "Margaret always wanted children, but I guess God willed otherwise. I was indifferent. It didn't really matter to me, other than that Maggie was disappointed. Then last week a blinding light flashed and I was struck from my horse on the road to Damascus."

"And what did you learn?"

"That a man has to give in this life."

"But you *have* given. To Margaret."

"Well, yes. And, God knows, I've given to the army. But I'm not talking about that. I mean giving to someone younger. To someone who'll replace you someday."

"I think we all have that need. Some of us just deny it."

"That river was dammed for half a century. Then I looked across the street at those rosy cheeks and that smile and the dam cracked. The flood just came crashing out."

"Let it."

"A colonel in the army can't afford that loss of control."

"Yes he can. Within these walls no one else need know. You're safe here."

No answer came.

"She adores you, Mac."

"I know." His voice sounded strange. "And I don't know why."

I could have sworn his voice was cracking. How could he be so upset?

"Why ask why?" mother said. "It doesn't matter. Why is the most useless word in the English language."

He laughed softly, and I was relieved to hear that. "You're not allowed to be wiser than I. You're too much younger."

"Not all that much."

A silence followed that seemed to last a week.

Finally Mac said, "Thank you for sharing your daughter with me, Mrs. Malone."

"I share her with very few."

"I realize that."

"Oh, Red, come here and sit by me. . . ."

My heart started pounding.

Silence, and then, "I don't think that's a good idea, Mary."

"All right," she said softly.

I heard him get up. "Time for this trooper to pitch his tent."

The floor creaked, and then it stopped.

"One thing about today," he said. "What do you know about Skeels?"

Mother groaned. "He's the most horrible man alive. The story is that he's the catch colt of a cattle thief and a poor Mexican girl. Apparently he didn't know either of them. She died when he was very young. He raised himself in the alleys of El Paso. He's a scalphunter."

"That explains the skinning knife."

"Supposedly he's sold dozens of Apache scalps to the Mexicans. Women, babies, he makes no distinction. The rumor is that when he runs out of Indians, he just kills Mexicans and sells their scalps. Have you seen him before?"

"No, but after you serve out here for decades, you get to know things even though you don't know why you know them.

Apacheria

You become intuitive in order to survive. That happened again today."

I heard him walk toward his room.

"Wait, Mac. What do you mean?"

He stopped. "I realized this afternoon that someday I'm going to have to kill Alejandro Skeels. Or he's going to kill me. Good night, Mary. Keep that little girl safe."

I bolted toward the bed. I slid under the sheet and faced away from mother's side. I breathed slowly and heavily so she would think I was in a deep sleep.

Instead of undressing, she knelt beside her edge of the bed. I knew she was praying to the Blessed Mother. She always prayed to her namesake when most in need. She had taught me to seek Mary's help whenever I was uncertain or fearful—or tempted. Then she stood up and leaned across the bed and kissed me on the cheek.

"Good night, sweetheart." Her voice was cheerful and, I think, relieved. "Don't try to fool your mommy."

Then she began humming to herself pleasantly as she got undressed.

10

The mid-morning sun was streaming through the window when I woke up. I had not slept so late in years. I jumped out of bed and washed and dressed as quickly as I could. I ran into the parlor, but the house was empty. Mother had long since gone to our store. I went outside and was happy to see Reba. She stood in the shade of a cottonwood near her end of the corral and was swishing at flies with her tail.

"Hi, Mac!" I shouted.

He waved to me from the far end of the stable. He looked like he had just finished the morning cleaning. As an officer, he probably had not mucked horsehocky in decades. Yet he seemed to be enjoying it. By the time I was five years old, I had learned that cleaning and feeding and watering horses was an act of simple purity like no other. It was a task so basic and raw that one could not wedge beneath it. Here was the primal starting point from which man and beast began their journey together. And it was exhilarating.

Voices from the other side of the house startled me. I hurried around the porch to see Pino and his men hard at work erecting the casita. I was surprised to see that one of them was Timmy. He was covered with sweat and dust, but when he saw me he seemed the happiest boy alive. Pino grinned, too, as I walked over. Pino was one of those people who needed a reason *not* to smile. He was very dark-skinned with salt-and-pepper hair and he was burly like a wrestler. His clothes always looked as if they had just been picked from the rag bin. I doubted he had a shirt that was not torn. And never had there been a hairier Mexican. His back showed through several rips in his shirt, and he looked like he was wearing a mohair sweater underneath. He was one of those men with a talent for everything and could turn his hand to any task. And always with a smile. Easterners who came to Arizona with silly notions about Mexicans wailing mournful serenades in the moonlight were always shocked by Pino, who laughed at everything and was grateful for every breath. If you were in need, he would give you his last tortilla or the shirt off his back. Even a torn one. I liked him immensely.

He waved to me as I wandered over. He told Timmy to take a break. Timmy wiped away the sweat that was running into his eyes and took the ladle and helped himself to some water from the pail nearby. Then we sat in the shade of the porch.

"The colonel is paying me three times what I make at the stable," he said.

I smiled but my heart was not in it. "You work too much, Timmy."

"I can't work too much. Someday I'll have a wife and children to provide for."

It seemed silly to me for a thirteen-year-old to talk about something like that. But he was so sincere that I just said, "Whoever catches you will be a lucky girl."

He looked at me in surprise. I had never noticed before how expressive his dark brown eyes were. And it was a nice feeling that washed over me as he gazed at me.

"I know that's a long way off," he said, turning away, "but I'll be ready."

I started to feel uncomfortable. It was a pleasing discomfort that I could not understand.

"I have to go now," I said.

"Thanks for coming over." He acted as if five minutes of my time were the most valuable thing in the world.

I wandered away and wondered if life could get any more confusing.

Reba and Dollar were saddled up when I got to the other side of the house.

"I want to talk with the sheriff, Katy. Go get your hat."

I raced into the house for my new hat and got back in time to see Mac sliding his Springfield carbine into the saddle scabbard.

"Let's ride," he said, and we mounted and were off.

When we arrived in town, Mac said he would see me in a little while. I took that to mean that this was man's work and I was not to tag along. So I went to our mercantile to see if mother needed help with anything.

There were a few customers in the store, but mother was not there. I went to the back room and was surprised to see Nahbay and Ishke, my two Indian friends, seated at the table with mother. They greeted me as cheerfully as if they had not seen me in a year. They were brother and sister and lived in a shack on the ragged edge of Mr. Devlin's land. He had always had a warm spot for them, and he let them live there in return for labor. They had no family of their own.

Mother looked troubled. "I don't know what to tell you. I can't afford to hire you and . . . there aren't many jobs in town these days."

What she really meant was that no one wanted to hire them. To many people, they were worse than ordinary Apaches because they were actually half-bloods. Their father was a German silver prospector, but, as the saying goes, they favored their mother. One would never guess they were half white. But just the knowledge that they were half-bloods seemed to infuriate people. I could never understand that. It angered me and baffled me.

"But I can do any kind of work," Nahbay said.

He did not exaggerate. He was about thirty and looked strong enough to bend railroad spikes. Ishke was twenty-five or so and was as lovely and clever as he was powerful.

Apacheria

"We will do any chore that needs to be done," Ishke said. "We turn our backs on nothing."

"I know," mother said.

She looked terribly torn. I think she would have considered emptying her bank account for them if it had been worth emptying.

"Lomaddis has given us no time," Nahbay said. "The day Mr. Devlin leaves, we have to be off the land."

"I hate him!" I shouted.

"Katy! Enough of that." Mother ran a hand across her forehead. I knew that it was always a sign of despair. "I'll ask around and see if I can find something for you."

"Thank you," Ishke said.

"Why don't you go over to the hotel now and have a meal? Katy go with them and tell Mr. Rice to put it on my bill."

"We want no charity," Nahbay said.

"It's a gift," mother answered, her eyes as stern as any Apache's.

Ishke touched her brother's arm. "Thank you, Mrs. Malone."

I took them to the Paradise and led them to our table. I told Mr. Rice that they were to have whatever they wanted.

On the way out, I saw Lomaddis and Skeels and Scabby coming toward the hotel. I quickly got out of the way and pushed them from my mind in order to save myself another trip to Confession.

Mother was still sitting at the table in the back room and looking as pained as when I left.

"Don't worry," I said. "We'll find something to help them."

"Why does everyone always expect me to fix things?" she said in exasperation. "I'm nobody special."

"Mommy, if there were lepers in this town, they'd come to you to be healed."

She could not help smiling at me. "Katy, Katy, you're my light in the darkness. You're" — she laughed — "you have no idea what I'm talking about, do you?"

I shook my head no.

"That's all right." She reached across the table and squeezed my hands. "What's Mac up to today?"

"He's with Sheriff Blaine."

"Jim is out of town."

"Then I guess he's on his way here. I'll go meet him."

When I got out onto the street, I knew right away something was wrong. Hooting and shouting from the Paradise made no sense. Those were barroom sounds. I ran across the street and into the lobby. It was deserted. A crowd clogged the entrance to the dining room. I knew something terrible was happening. I threw myself at the crowd and elbowed people out of the way and even kicked some of them. They were too startled to object but not too proud to yelp as I gouged my way through.

"Rice, since when do you serve breeds?" Lomaddis was saying.

Mr. Rice dared not object with Skeels' skinning knife at his throat.

Scabby stood off to the right.

The plates of food in front of Nahbay and Ishke had been dumped over onto the table. They glared at their tormentors, but they knew they were powerless here.

"You worthless pile of trash!" I shouted at Lomaddis.

"Wooh!" Skeels said. "Look at that little redhead."

Lomaddis laughed. "Just like her mother."

"We're just having some fun," Scabby said.

"This isn't fun, Norbert."

"Shut up before I spank you," Lomaddis said. He turned back to my friends. "Do you know the problem with you Apaches? You're too grim. You need some sweetening."

He took the bowl of strawberry preserves from the table and dumped the contents onto Nahbay's head. Ishke leaped up at Lomaddis, but Nahbay held her back.

"What do you think?" Lomaddis said.

The sticky red mess began running down Nahbay's face.

"*Muy dulce!*" Skeels said with a laugh.

Apacheria

"It's not a complete meal, though." Lomaddis picked up a tub of butter and a knife.

"That's enough, Clete," Scabby said.

"Never enough." Lomaddis spread a smear of butter across each of Nahbay's cheekbones. "Looks like war paint. Hard to believe people could ever be afraid of garbage like this."

Nahbay stared up at him. I was shocked to see no anger on his face. I realized that he was long past that now. His sad eyelids hung as heavy as shrouds over the tragedy and hopelessness of a fallen race.

"Good work, Clete," a voice behind me said.

Lomaddis smiled and turned and looked beyond me.

I heard a grunt of exertion. A coffee cup shot like a comet across the room and exploded in the center of Clete's forehead and he collapsed like a bag of rocks.

A powerful arm hooked around me and pulled me out of harm's way. I knew at once who it was.

Mac strode into the dining room.

Skeels lowered his knife from Mr. Rice's neck and Scabby backed off.

Lomaddis pushed himself to his feet, blood running down his face from the ugly wound in his head. He was unarmed, and so was Mac.

Then Lomaddis charged.

Mac stepped aside as neatly as a matador. Mac's right fist smashed into Lomaddis's left cheekbone and his knees buckled and he went down. He was now at Mac's mercy. But Mac held back.

With his chest heaving, Lomaddis managed to get to his feet.

Mac waited.

"No, Clete!" Scabby yelled.

But Lomaddis was beyond reason now. The punch he threw had no steel in it and Mac swatted it aside indifferently. Then Mac's left hand shot out and closed around his throat.

Lomaddis's arms were shorter than Mac's, so all he could do was flail helplessly as Mac's fist crashed into the center of his mouth. His lips were crushed, but Mac punched him again. Two more times in quick succession he hit him, and then again and yet again. Lomaddis's lips had lost all shape, shredded against his own teeth. Another hammer strike, and then another, but still Mac's fury could not be sated. Lomaddis's legs were rubber now, but Mac held him up. He hurled another titanic blow, and I heard teeth crack and Mac let him fall.

I was terrified Mac had killed him, but my soldier knew his trade. Half-conscious, Lomaddis lay coiled on himself like a maggot tossed onto a hot stone.

Mac turned toward Skeels. "Today? Or later?"

Skeels sheathed his knife. "Another day."

Skeels left the room with Scabby close behind.

Mac turned to me. He looked sad that I had witnessed this, as though I might think that this frightening side was all there was to him. But there was no cause for that. I knew there were many Macs. He was the respected commander of Captain Colton. The inscrutable ally of Sheriff Blaine. The alarmingly attractive older man of my lonely mother. But this Mac? This one was mine. He was the strong man of my hidden yearnings. Tough and implacable and roused to righteous rage. Indifferent to his safety when protecting those weaker than himself—even people he had warred against and sometimes killed. He was the stalwart masculine guardian I had never known but for whom I had always secretly hungered. No, there was nothing for him to apologize for. This—this above all—was *my* Mac, and he was mine alone.

11

"I want their heads!" Sheriff Blaine said.

"Let it go, Jim," Mac answered in a soothing voice.

Mother pushed Mac's swollen hand back into a bowl of cool water. "Keep it there."

"What's the point?" Mac said to Jim. "Lomaddis has his punishment. And Skeels and Scabby could claim that it was just a prank that got out of hand."

"What about the knife at Rice's throat?"

"Do you think he'll swear out a complaint against Skeels? Why should he risk that? If Skeels and Lomaddis aren't back shooters, I'm a Dutchman. And besides, Skeels will say it was a joke. And nobody will convict him for humiliating a couple of Indians."

Jim turned to Nahbay and Ishke sitting at the far side of our back room. "Will you help me with this?"

Mac said something to them in Indeh before they could answer.

"It is finished," Nahbay finally said to Jim.

"Why would anyone want to be sheriff in this town?" Jim said, shaking his head.

Mac smiled. "Look at it this way. It lessens your time in Purgatory."

"It builds me a mansion in Heaven."

He turned away in frustration and left the store.

"Dry your hand," mother said, giving Mac a towel.

She opened a jar of balm.

"What is that?" Mac asked.

"Horse lineament."

"Appropriate for a horse soldier."

She smeared some on the back of his hand and tenderly rubbed it into his knuckles.

"Pay attention, Katy," Mac said. "You might have to do this for a foolish husband someday."

"Oh, shut up!" mother shouted.

Mac looked at her in astonishment, and so did I.

"There were three of them for Heaven's sake. You could've been killed."

"Should I have left these people to those scum?"

"No, no, I don't mean that. You should have gotten help."

"And who in this town could I have relied on? Other than you and Katy. And she tried to face Lomaddis down"—he winked at me—"but Fireball here is still a little too short for that."

"We are very grateful, colonel," Nahbay said.

"I understand you and your sister are looking for work."

"Yes."

"I'm building a casita on Mrs. Malone's property. Do you know the place?"

"Yes."

"Go there and tell Pino I sent you. Give him a hand and I'll pay you what's fair."

"Thank you, colonel. We will go at once."

He and Ishke hurried off.

Mac scowled at the lineament. "Not the greatest smell in the world."

Mother gave him an annoyed look but kept on rubbing. She seemed like she would have massaged his hand all day.

"May I come in?"

We turned to the doorway and saw Padre Tomas standing there.

Apacheria

"Come in, Father," mother said, releasing Mac's hand and giving him the towel. "Have a seat."

He removed his hat and joined us.

"I heard what happened at the hotel."

"Everybody has heard what happened at the hotel," Mac said. "Not much excitement in this town."

"I came to thank you for what you did."

"Well, I didn't expect that from a man of the cloth."

"Justified anger is not a sin. Nor is striking a blow for the innocent." He looked down at Mac's hand. "Or even many blows."

"Thank you, Padre."

"And thank you for speaking up for the Apaches yesterday."

"I didn't speak up for them. And I didn't speak against them. I spoke the facts. That's all."

"I think you know what I mean."

"Just so we understand each other, what happened at the hotel was trivial compared to what might happen very soon."

"I fear that is true."

"I've killed more Apaches than you have fingers and toes. If I see Manolete within a hundred yards of Mrs. Malone or her daughter, I'll cut him down without a second thought. Without compunction and without remorse."

"I understand that." He reached into the pocket of his cassock and took out a small red flannel pouch. "Do you know that St. Michael is the patron saint of soldiers?"

"I do."

The padre opened the pouch and pulled out a silver medal of the great archangel. "Have you ever prayed to him."

"Every day. For many years."

I looked at mother. More than admiration filled her eyes. Something much deeper.

"I would like you to have this medal and wear it in safety."

Mac suddenly lost his edge. He seemed deeply moved.

"Thank you, Father."

"Before I give it to you, I would like to bless it with a little prayer I wrote a while ago." He held it in his left palm and extended his right hand over it. "Michael, Prince of the Heavenly Host by the power of God, defend this man with your shield, inspire him with your honor, refresh him with your strength, comfort him with your love. In his hour of need, let the drawn sword of your righteousness imbue him with the valor of all the legions of Heaven, so that he may confront every evil with a steadfast heart. And, finally, conduct him and those he loves into the presence of Almighty God, where together they may share blessed peace and joy forever. Through Christ Our Lord. Amen."

He took the chain and reached across and looped it over Mac's head. Then he stood up. "God bless you all."

"Bye, Father," I said.

He smiled and laid his hand on my head and gave me a blessing in Latin. And then he left as quietly as he had come.

"Moral courage is rare in this town," mother said, watching him go.

"Moral courage is rare in any town," Mac said.

Mother was jittery, an odd state for her.

"You'd better have a brandy, Mary."

She squeezed her hands together to keep them still. "I don't know how Margaret endured it."

"Margaret?" he said in surprise.

The startled look on mother's face was priceless when she suddenly realized she had put herself in the place of Mac's wife.

"I mean . . . it's just that . . . how did she stand it? The danger I mean. Of your job."

Mac had an amused look on his face as he allowed her to stumble along.

"She was steel." He looked at mother meaningfully. "It's been my good fortune to know several women like that."

"It's just that you've got me so worried now."

"Why? Worry is a useless effort. If it weren't, why would people have to do it so often?"

Apacheria

She turned away, still clasping her hands together.

"Life was simpler before, wasn't it?" he said.

"Before what?"

"Before me."

"Don't say that! It's not what I meant."

"It's exactly what you meant. But it's all right."

She sighed and shook her head. "Do you have any idea how much I admire Margaret?"

And envy her she could have said, but dared not.

"Yes, I do," Mac answered. He looked at me and then back at mother. "And Maggie would have envied you as well."

"I didn't say envy," she shot back. "I said admire."

"Yes." His smile had an odd hint of sadness in it, as if he regretted bringing turmoil into our lives.

"I just feel overwhelmed right now." She turned away and stared at nothing. "It'll pass."

"Maybe I made a mistake."

"What mistake?"

"Stopping to water my horse."

She squeezed her hands together again but said nothing.

"I think it's time for me to go."

He slid out his chair and stood up.

Mother spun around so quickly I jumped with a start and almost fell backward off my chair.

"Go where?!"

The look of panic in her eyes seemed to shock Mac.

"To check on Pino to see how he's coming along with the casita."

"Oh . . . yes. That's a good idea. I'll be back soon. I'm going to close the store early today."

"Keep an eye on her, Fireball," he said to me with a wink. "Your commanding officer is a bit rattled today."

After Mac left, mother told me to man the counter while she went for a walk. She was back soon, though, and said she was going home. I was to stay open until noon and then close for the

day.

Two of my girlfriends came in shortly afterward and wanted to go do girly things, but I told them I had to be at the store. I was glad I had the excuse. So many of the things that had excited me a week earlier seemed small and silly to me now.

I put the honor box on the counter and took a pen and the ink bottle and some sheets of paper and went to the back room. I began writing down everything that had happened this day. My hand was tired by the time I finished that part, but I kept writing, going back to Friday and continuing to last night. I was determined this would be the best diary ever. Little did I know it would eventually form the basis of much more.

I decided not to go directly home after I had closed our mercantile. I rode out to the San Pedro, one of my favorite places in the world. Of course, at that time my world was very small, but even as I write these words now there is still no place that soothes me like the valley of the San Pedro.

Lush is not a word that most people associate with Arizona. So the river valley always startles them. The dry grasslands were right to hand, and even the forbidding harshness of the Sonoran Desert was not far away. Yet here all was green. And not just the green of the mesquites and the clumps of bunch grass, though there were plenty of those. The towering cottonwoods loomed over all in a great canopy that cooled and refreshed. More birds than one could ever imagine gave song here. Lizards scurried during the day and toads croaked in the evening. Bobcats could occasionally be glimpsed, especially at dusk. And for the stoutest of souls that rarest of treats, the large prints of a jaguar pressed into the mud as he patrolled silently along the bank.

Most horses did not like to be here. The dense tree stands made it hard for them to see, and the endless rustling of the cottonwoods confused their hearing. Yet Dollar was more tolerant than most, because I had trained him to be. It was not

easy being my horse, or my friend. I knew that. I demanded a lot. One of the reasons I was so glad Timmy had punched Billy Boy Scarns was that I was secretly afraid that nasty boy was right. I was different from most girls. A filly who always fought the halter. But mother usually made sure to give me plenty of lead line. She jerked me back only when she thought it was really necessary. Naturally, I believed it was never necessary and was completely uncalled for. One of my dearest hopes was that someday she would at last become as wise as I was. If I could get there in eleven years, it made no sense to me that it was taking her more than thirty.

Dollar stood in the mud and dipped his lips into the water and refreshed himself. I sat on an ancient mesquite limb, long since snapped and dead and embedded now in the bank.

I looked up the quiet river and imagined its origins hundreds of miles away in the mountains of Mexico. It seemed silly to me that people often thought of rivers as barriers. They were nothing of the kind. This gorgeous flow of water was like a giant blood vessel pumping life into the land. Birds and fish and cats and bugs and snakes all flowed with it. And sometimes even people. Dangerous people, too. I knew it was unwise to linger here, but I could not keep away. And besides, my guardian angel was always with me.

I took Dollar's reins and we walked south along the bank. Unseen animals scampered and splashed before us. I strained to glimpse a salamander or toad in the dappled sunlight. So focused was I that it was not until I gave up and relaxed that I saw something much larger right before me. Hoofprints fresh and clean beneath my feet. They were headed north, so the horses had already passed the spot where I was, maybe just a few minutes before I had gotten to the river. I bent down. The prints were still sharp and clear, with just a few flecks of mud crumbling off the inner edges. But most ominous of all was the fact that these were unshod horses.

I tried to tell myself that my heart was not pounding. My

mouth was dry, but I did not want to bother with my canteen. I mounted Dollar and rode back the way we had walked. Dollar raised his head and his ears caught something before mine did. Splashing hoofbeats sounded down the bank and were growing louder and coming toward us. I looked behind me, but I did not want to go south. Who knew what might lurk there? I nudged Dollar to the left away from the bank, but he balked at the tangle of mesquites.

"Oh, Dollar," I said and laid the rein across his neck and kicked him hard with both heels.

He tried to make it through, but he was smarter than I about this. There was nowhere to go.

"Mary, mother of God," I whispered, and then I saw the most beautiful sight on earth, Reba's sorrel face bursting through the shadows.

"Mac!"

I raced toward him and pulled up alongside. He had his sidearm on his hip and his Springfield in its scabbard.

"Katy, you shouldn't be here alone. What are you doing out here? " His voice was not kind.

"Just being by myself. How did you know where I was?"

"Timmy said you come here."

I think if I had been five years old, he would have spanked me right then.

"I saw hoofprints back there, Mac. Heading north. Unshod ponies."

He gazed beyond my shoulder and nodded. "How many mounts?"

"It was too much of a jumble for me to be sure. But more than half a dozen, I think."

"All right, let's head home."

"Wait," I said before he could turn Reba around. "Please."

He gave me a look that made mother's stern glare seem like a grin. "What is it?"

"Please don't tell mother about this. I can't bear to be kept at home."

Apacheria

"Is that how she punishes you?"

"Yes," I said meekly.

"Well, as I see it, you just conducted a scout and reported the information back to your colonel. That's a confidential matter between two officers and nothing more need be said about it. Now let's go."

Reba pivoted as if she had read his mind, and they were off, with me and Dollar right behind them.

The lump in my throat was as big as my fist. Mother was right. My God, how I adored him.

12

Fort Huachuca is younger than I am. It was started only in '77. Then it was just a camp, but soon a full-size fort provided a regiment to protect the settlements flung across the southeastern part of the territory.

Easterners were usually disappointed the first time they saw a fort without walls. They expected a timber palisade of sharply pointed poles and watch towers and whatnot. As if the Apaches were stupid enough to mount an attack against a massive military encampment. In fact, the fort seemed almost relaxed in its arrangement, with the buildings casually sprawled out on the flats and up to and occasionally on the surrounding hills.

That morning at breakfast, Mac had asked me if I wanted to visit the fort. I was thrilled at the chance, but I was old enough to know that the excursion was not simply to entertain me.

Now we sat on our horses at the edge of the parade ground. I was wearing the hat Mac had bought me and the neckerchief he had given me that first day. Mac's only concession to his former life was his buff campaign hat. He wore a dark blue bib shirt and plain black trousers.

We watched some of the horse soldiers exercising their mounts and putting them through some basic maneuvers. We had little time to do that, though, because word of Mac's presence spread fast. Captain Colton came running up.

"Looking for a job, colonel?" he said with a grin.

Apacheria

"Not with this pack of desert dogs. We came by to see the colonel."

"I think he's in his quarters, sir."

"Is Mrs. Hargrave here?"

"I believe she's in Washington at the moment, sir."

"Ask the colonel if he'll receive us."

Colton gave a casual salute and ran across the parade ground to a modest adobe building situated at the edge of it.

Some of the troopers on the field recognized Mac and raced over to greet him. Soon the maneuvers were forgotten and we were surrounded by horsemen. They joked and laughed with Mac, and it was clear how happy they were to see him.

"Those moves out there looked sloppy," he said in a half-serious tone. "Don't you want to please your new commander?"

"He can't be pleased, sir," one of the troopers said.

I looked at Mac. His expression was suddenly serious but he did not reply.

"Let him through!" I heard Colton shout as he ran up.

Some of the troopers reined their horses aside.

"The colonel will receive you now, sir," Colton said.

"Maybe I'll see some of you saddle tramps on the way out," Mac said. "If I can't avoid it."

The men laughed and hooted. We rode through them and made our way across the parade ground.

A middle-aged Mexican woman greeted us at the door of the adobe house. She took our hats and showed us into a small parlor. I was surprised at what a modest place it was. The most elaborate piece of furniture was a well worn red brocade chesterfield nearing the end of its earthly life. A few white wicker chairs with pillows were arranged near it to form a small seating area. Prints and brightly colored Mexican blankets decorated the walls, and tall vases of dried flowers were tucked into the corners. Through an archway I could see a dining room with a lace-covered table and four chairs. A small china closet sat against the far wall and was flanked by a pair of bookcases. A

tiny iron stove at the right side of the room was ready to take the edge off winter nights and stop supper from getting cold too fast.

We heard a door close somewhere in the back of the house and our host soon came striding through the dining room and into the parlor. He smiled when he saw Mac. For reasons I could not explain, I felt that he had not smiled much lately.

"Well, well, Redmond McGregor," he said and came forward and shook Mac's hand.

"How are you, Jack?"

"Passable. And this young lady?"

"Katherine Malone. I'm staying with Katherine and her mother."

"I see," he said, looking down at me, for he was very tall. "I'll bet it's Katy then."

I smiled. "Yes, sir." I reached out to shake his hand.

He took hold of my fingers and bent in a graceful bow and kissed the back of my hand. "*Enchanté*."

I felt myself blushing.

"Please have a seat," he said.

I sat on the chesterfield and Mac joined me. Colonel Hargrave sat on a wicker chair across from us.

The colonel was a few years younger than Mac and very trim. Short steel-gray hair gave him a burnished appearance, as did his neatly cut silver moustache. The lines in his lean face marked it with a taut masculinity any man could envy.

"I understand Jane is back East," Mac said.

"Her mother is unwell."

"I'm sorry to hear that."

"She'll be disappointed she missed you. She's always been very fond of you, you know."

"No accounting for taste," Mac said with a laugh.

The Mexican woman came in with a tray holding a pitcher of lemonade and some glasses and a plate of pecan biscuits. She set it down on a small table near the chesterfield.

Apacheria

"I'd offer you something stiffer," the colonel said to Mac, "but I know the soul of the agave is one you reserve for sundown."

"You've always had the best tequila."

"I have a friend in the Mexican Army. He has it shipped to me straight from Jalisco. I'll give you a bottle to take with you."

Mac seemed touched. Perhaps Colonel Hargrave was not known for gift giving.

"Thank you, Jack."

Hargrave poured me some lemonade and then some for Mac and himself.

"So what brings the old eagle back to his roost?"

Mac sipped his lemonade. "Care to guess?"

"Manolete."

"Any news?"

"None."

"No sign at all?"

"Not so far. Two daily scouts up and down the river but not a trace."

"Just yesterday I saw —," I started to say, but Mac held up his hand and I was quiet.

"Martinez's contacts in the *rurales*...?"

"Nothing."

"Do we even know why he broke out in the first place?"

"Possibly." Hargrave took a sip of his drink and set the glass onto the table. "I sent Colton up to San Carlos to see what he could find. He has a way with people. But the agent shriveled like a cactus in June. Didn't know a thing. Indian agents are the only people I know who love to revel in their own ignorance."

"No clues then?"

"One. Colton talked with some of the Apaches. They told him that the young wife of Manolete's brother had just died. Probably from eating some bad beef. He broke out right after that. He's probably sitting in the Sierra Madre now and plotting revenge."

"Manolete is not a forgiving man."

"I realize that. And you know him far better than I do."

"No reports of any depredations in Mexico?"

"Stock stealing but no killings yet."

"Very odd. Especially for him."

"It's strange. Rather late in life for a character change."

"That's not the issue, Jack. Make no mistake, Manolete is a man of exceptional character, if he's anything at all."

"I don't understand how you can say that." Hargrave seemed annoyed. "How can you believe such a thing?"

"Because it's true."

"I've never gotten your outlook on the Apaches."

"That they're an honorable people? Manolete never broke his word in his life. How many whites can you say that about?"

He looked even more annoyed. "That's not what I mean."

But it was clear that was what he did mean.

"You think I overestimate them?" Mac said.

"Sometimes."

"Even if that's true, what does it matter? If I overestimate them, it's just a foible. But if you underestimate them, it's a disaster."

"I know," Hargrave said with a sigh. "And I can't even figure out what that bastard wants." He looked at me. "I apologize for my language, young lady."

"Has Crook been down here?" Mac asked.

"In spirit. I feel him looking over my shoulder every second. He sent word he wants this settled. He doesn't want to have to go down into the Sierra Madre again like he did for that drunken idiot Geronimo."

"He doesn't want you to cross the border, does he?"

"Preferably not."

"Then all you can do is wait."

"Crook is not a patient man." Hargrave got up. "He always liked you, so put a good word in for me if he stops by for afternoon tea."

Apacheria

Hargrave went over to the window and locked his hands behind his back and stared out across the parade ground.

"What's the matter, Jack?"

"I've got problems, Red." He kept gazing out the window. "I don't think I was meant for this."

"Are you joking? You were born for this."

"That's the problem. It's always been assumed. I assumed it myself. And you knew my father."

"Only slightly."

"He fought in the Mexican War."

"Vera Cruz, wasn't it?"

"Yes. He won so many medals it's a wonder he could stand up straight."

"You've done him proud."

A long silence followed and finally he said, "I think not."

"I don't understand."

Hargrave turned and looked at Mac. "I'd make a fine staff officer. I'm sure of that. But I'm not a field commander. And I can't become one just because I've read Upton. I'm in trouble here, Red. I don't have the knack."

"For what?"

"The men."

"Ah...."

Hargrave came back to his chair and sat down. "I'm on the brink of a terrible failure. I was raised and groomed for this my whole life. And now it's about to fall to ashes."

Mac sipped his lemonade and helped himself to a biscuit. "Do you want advice, or do you just want to wander around this fort and feel sorry for yourself?"

Anger flashed in Hargrave's eyes, but it quickly vanished. He seemed to realize that Mac had deliberately goaded him.

"I'll take the advice."

Mac set down his glass. "Do you know one of the most common mistakes a commander makes? He thinks of his men as soldiers instead of his soldiers as men. You have to remember

they struggle with a thousand little needs and a thousand giant weaknesses every day of their lives. You've read Caesar, haven't you?"

"Many times."

"Read him again. No man understood soldiers better. Ignore Napoleon and Wellington. They had contempt for their men. But go back to the great Roman. You know Latin, so read him in the original. I haven't been anywhere in the last thirty years that my copy of the *Commentaries* hasn't been with me."

The first truly warm smile softened the colonel's face. "Do you know I envy you?"

"Don't be ridiculous."

"All these years I've strained to be the ideal officer."

"You try too hard."

"I know. I've always known. But you—it just flows naturally."

"I went to the Point after the War. You know that."

Hargrave laughed. "The Point never taught you anything you didn't already know. How could it? All the battles you'd fought in. . . . And then the Medal of Honor. Stones River, wasn't it?"

"That doesn't matter. It's now that's important."

"My now is very precarious."

"It doesn't have to be. You need to form a partnership with your men. And I don't mean just the officers."

"What are you talking about? I can't fraternize with the troops."

"You're too European, Jack. They created that caste system. And it's good, but you can't make it a religion."

"You think I should bend it?"

"Of course. You'll never be an enlisted man's friend and you shouldn't try. If every officer did that, the army would fall apart. But you can be a doting uncle."

"I've never thought of myself as that."

"You'd better start."

"And how would you go about it?"

Apacheria

"Well, the best examples I can think of are the Ninth and Tenth."

"You're joking."

"Am I?"

"What do colored regiments have to do with me?"

"Everything. They have the highest morale. And the fewest desertions. Why do you think that is?"

"I can't say I ever gave it any thought."

"It's because outside the army, those men are at everybody's mercy—just niggers to be beaten or robbed or lynched. But inside the army, they're men and they're patriots. They have rank and standing and meaning."

"But how does that apply to white troops? Most of them could do better outside the army. At least in terms of money."

"Exactly. So you have to go past money."

"How?"

"By reinforcing for them the standing and dignity of an American soldier—regardless of salary. What it means to wear blue. And you have to offer them what they crave most. What the colored soldiers need and what all men crave—security from injustice and pain."

"They know I try to be fair."

"It goes beyond that. You have to be shelter against the storm, whatever the cost to you or your career."

"I try to, but it doesn't come naturally to me."

"Nothing worth doing is easy."

"I don't even know where to begin that kind of approach."

"Forget the grand gesture. It's the small things that matter to soldiers."

"Such as?"

"Food is a good start. Supplement the commissary out of your own pocket. I always did. Don't let the men suffer with army slop. Feed these men well and they'll walk on hot coals for you."

Hargrave smiled. "I can do that."

"Address them directly. I've been in outfits where officers never spoke to their men except through the First Sergeant. Don't make that mistake."

"I've tried but they seem uneasy."

"Do it anyway. Walk into the barracks some night and sit on a footlocker and tell them to fire up a pot of black jack. They'll be stunned at first. Yet when they realize that you're there for no reason except to see how they're doing, they'll soften like butter in the sun."

"You make it sound easy."

"It's not as hard as you think. And if you really want to melt them, throw some money on a bunk and tell them to break out the cards."

The colonel stared at Mac as if he were insane. "I have a rule against gambling in the barracks."

"I know you do. That's why you have to break it — *with them*. You can't imagine the effect this will have. And make sure you lose a few big hands."

Hargrave looked as if he were about to say something but then apparently thought better of it.

"And one more thing," Mac said. "Make sure you don't rescind the rule against gambling. If you do, the men will be happy for five minutes, but they'll lose respect for you. Keep it in force."

"But then I'd be breaking a rule I made myself."

"That's the power of it. Every month or so on a Saturday night stroll in and toss your money down. Show them that sometimes you hate rules, too, and get fed up with them as much as they do."

Hargrave could not help laughing, and I was surprised that it was really a very pleasant laugh.

"Believe me, Jack, if you do that, they're yours forever. Thirty years from now, they'll tell their grandchildren about the patrician colonel who broke his own commandment and spent an evening with them. Who gambled his money across an old army blanket in a barracks in the Arizona Territory."

Hargrave smiled at Mac. "The men miss you, Red."

"They have to get over it. *You* have to be their bulwark now. Like the white officers with their black troops. They'd die for their men and those men would die for them."

"Commanding the Tenth hasn't exactly helped Grierson's career, though. You know him, don't you?"

"Very well. One of the finest officers there is."

"I heard that Sheridan doesn't care for him."

"Of course he doesn't. Nobody likes the Negroes' officers. And that pompous little windbag doesn't like anyone who isn't a narrow-minded sycophant like he is."

The colonel nodded. "I miss Sherman."

"We all miss Sherman. It was a sad day when he retired. So many people think he's the spawn of the Devil. He can say the most savage things sometimes. But that's just steam. Underneath he's a wise and reasonable man."

"Like you, you crazy Celt." Hargrave smiled and pointed to Mac's swollen hand. "You'll never change."

Mac flexed his fingers a few times. "A minor disagreement."

"I'd hate to see his face."

Mac laughed. "Well, I did hear he threw away all his mirrors."

"I'm really glad you came today, even if I didn't have much information to offer about our Apache friend." Hargrave looked at me. "And you also, young lady. And I like that neckerchief."

I smiled at him. "Thank you, sir."

"Katy has excellent taste," Mac said.

"Are you going to stop and see the men?"

"Just for a minute." Mac stood up and held out his hand. "It's always good to see you, Jack."

Hargrave shook Mac's hand gently. "And you, old friend."

The colonel had the Mexican woman get our hats and a bottle of tequila for Mac, and we were on our way.

Mac put the tequila in a saddle bag. "We're going up to the barracks," he said, and we started up the hill.

"You like him a lot, don't you, Mac?"

"We go back far together. When the world was young."

"But he's very different from you."

"Querida, you can't just like people who are the same as you."

"But don't you think that's easier?"

"Not for me," he said, laughing. "I prefer people different from me. One of me is enough. I certainly could never put up with myself. I don't know how you and your mom do it."

I slipped my right hand into his left one. "We can put up with you forever."

Mac gave me the same smile he had given me that first day on the street. "I know." He squeezed my fingers and winked. "Now let's go straighten out some crooked asses."

I grinned. I loved when he used an off-color word to me. It made me feel special and grown-up, with a bond between us that no one else shared.

Three enormous barracks ruled the hill at the northern edge of the parade ground. They were two stories high with pitched roofs, and their whitewashed clapboard made me squint in the bright sun. A porch ran along the lower level of each building and a veranda along the upper. Men were going in or out, but no one was lounging there.

The big central doorway had a balcony above it, and we stepped into the cool shade of this and went inside.

In the dark corridor, some young soldiers who did not know Mac looked at us curiously. Mac headed toward a room that noise was coming from, but he told me to wait in the hallway. I guess he wanted to make sure there were no half-dressed soldiers inside. An explosive greeting from the men rumbled out of the room, and Mac called me above the din.

He was sitting on the edge of a footlocker at the end of a bunk about halfway down the room. The men made space for me and I went in and sat next to him.

"Katy, these are what the War Department calls cavalrymen. Hard to believe, I know, but there it is."

Apacheria

The soldiers, all enlisted men, laughed and gathered around, sitting on bunks or standing about.

The barracks room was big, with cots between the windows against both long walls and a large open space down the middle. Round rifle racks on wheels were situated in the space. There was also a mobile rack with a brass fire extinguisher atop it, a pair of axes hanging beneath, and a ring of leather buckets dangling from the edge. Another wheeled table held a barrel of drinking water. An iron stove dominated the center of the room. On the far wall between two windows, a clock ticked off the long days on the Arizona frontier. The whole place smelled of wool and leather and men's sweat, but that no longer seemed unpleasant to me.

"It's a damn sight neater in here than it used to be," Mac said, looking at the tidy racks of clothes and gear on the wall above each man's cot.

"Hargrave is stricter than you were, colonel," a corporal answered.

"Good. All of you could stand to have your characters improved."

Some of them booed jokingly.

"So why haven't you brought in Manolete?" Mac asked.

"We can't find him, sir," one of the privates said.

"I wonder if this sad crew could find him if he was sitting big as life in a cantina in Tucson and drinking bad whiskey."

"We miss you, colonel," another of the corporals said. "Your tenderness and warmth."

They all laughed.

"Colonel, we believe Manolete is still in Sonora." This was from a gray-haired sergeant whose craggy face was a battle map of the Apaches wars. His voice was as pleasant as cinders crushed under a boot.

"Could be, Paddy," Mac said. "But who knows?"

"Are you here to teach Hargrave how to command a regiment, sir?" one of the younger privates said good-naturedly.

Mac snapped his head around and the soldier actually flinched. "What's that supposed to mean?"

The private looked like he was about to wet himself.

"That man was taking hits from rebel canister when you were still swinging from a tit."

I covered my mouth to hide my smile.

Mac swept the room with a glare that could have shattered glass. "You obey the officer, not the man. Remember that."

The stunned men stared at him in silence, but I saw a smile in the eyes of the old sergeant.

"If you don't like it here," Mac said, "transfer to the northern plains. Then you'll beg to come back as soon as the snow flies."

No one said anything.

"So get your asses in the saddle and move out. I'll be back in a month. If there's even the hint of a problem, you'll answer to me."

The gray-haired sergeant stepped forward. "Colonel . . ."

"Paddy."

"We love you, too, sir."

Mac eyed him for a moment, and then his face eased into a grin.

The men relaxed, but I could see they knew Mac had meant what he said.

"Listen, you saddle bums. Hargrave cares about you. He might not have the most delicate touch, but if you need to be wet-nursed, you're in the wrong business. Understand?"

"Yes, sir," several of them said.

"When I was your commander, I asked for nothing except loyalty to the regiment and the nation. But I'm asking something now. Help that man find the final fulfillment of his life. Do it for him or do it for me. I don't care. But do it."

He stood up.

The men sitting on bunks stood also, and those standing straightened from their slouches.

"Don't disappoint me." Mac pulled a gold piece from his pocket and tossed it onto the footlocker. "Firewater on me. Make it Irish." Then he grabbed his hat and headed to the door.

I walked behind him, and the soldiers, straight as arrows now, stepped aside to let us pass. Mac was out in the corridor and I was closing the barracks room door when I heard one of the men say, "Jesus Christ, I love that man."

I smiled and shut the door quietly and hurried after him.

13

Our owl began his nightly song while Mac and I sat on the porch step in the dark.

"I've always enjoyed the night," Mac said. "The quiet and the coolness and the sweet smell."

A breeze was blowing down the river valley and glided across us and fluttered our sleeves.

"I love our owl," I said. "It's my favorite nighttime sound."

"Do you know what mine is?" He looked over at me. I could just make him out in the faint light coming from the house behind us.

"No, what?"

"The sound of a train whistle in the distance in the middle of the night. The thought of the engineer driving that great engine through the wilderness. The fragile people inside trusting him and the iron animal to protect them on a journey through the darkness to a strange destination beyond." He paused, and then said, "And when I was little, I pretended it was no ordinary train." He smiled at me. "I imagined that it was God's train carrying people to Heaven."

I smiled because I knew what he meant about enjoying feeling protected. I leaned against him and he slid his arm around me.

"Mac . . . ?" I said after a while.

"Mmmm?"

Apacheria

"Are you going to be a scout for the army like Captain Colton suggested?"

"Oh, I don't know. Why?"

"If you do, will you live at the fort?"

"I'd be a civilian. I could live anywhere I want. But it definitely wouldn't be near the regiment I commanded. That would undercut Colonel Hargrave too much. The men would always be looking to me rather than him."

"I liked him."

"He's a good soldier. Brave as they come. But his father was a stern man. Demanded perfection. It's an awful burden."

"Do you miss the army?"

"I miss the routine I guess. Civilian life is too haphazard."

I was not sure what he meant by that, but I did not want to sound foolish by asking him.

"It isn't easy adjusting. Not at my age. Yet we're expected to. We reach the peak of our knowledge and skill, and then we quit and turn everything over to somebody else." He looked away and gazed into the night. "We're too young to sit on a porch and whittle, but too old to learn something new. Ridiculous when you stop to think about it."

I reached up and wrapped my fingers around his big hand resting on my shoulder.

"But aren't there new adventures?" I asked.

"Oh, yes," he said, and I could hear a smile in his voice. "Where you least expect it."

Mother came out onto the porch. Mac stood, as he always did when mother appeared, but she pressed a hand against his shoulder and he sat back down. She sat on the other side of him from me.

"Ishke and Nahbay are finishing the dishes," she said. "I told them they could stay in the barn for the night. I don't want them traveling in the dark."

"You're quite the mother hen," Mac said.

"I can cluck with the best of them," she answered with a

laugh.

"The casita will be finished in a few days," Mac said. "A nice little place for a couple of hired hands."

Mother looked out toward it, though it was invisible in the darkness. "I hadn't thought of that."

"You might want to consider it. They'll work cheap. And they might see it as a privilege to watch over the homestead of the celebrated Mrs. Malone."

"Oh, stop it."

"I like them, mommy."

"All right. I'll think abut it."

We were quiet for a spell, and then mother said, "You didn't speak much at supper about what happened at the fort today."

"There isn't much to say," Mac answered. "Nobody knows anything about what Manolete is up to."

Then he summarized what he and the colonel had talked about.

"It sounds pretty thin," mother said.

"Cobwebs."

"But you have some ideas, I'll bet."

"Katy told me once that you were a mind reader."

"So watch out!" she said. She seemed especially spirited and happy this night.

"I'll be careful," Mac said.

"So what about Manolete?"

"I think Jack Hargrave is wrong. Not about why Manolete bolted. That has the ring of truth. But about what his plans are."

"Then what are they?"

"I think he had none. He might be down in the Sierra Madre, but I don't believe he's sitting there planning killings."

"I don't understand," mother said.

"Manolete is a man of towering emotions. Terrifying rages. And he's a very keen judge of himself—a rare trait in any man. I think he bolted to *stop* himself from killing."

"But why?" she asked.

"Because he knows if he struck someone down, the government might take it out on all the Chiricahuas. There have been people pushing for that. Shipping them all off to Oklahoma or Alabama or Florida where they could never escape again."

"Would they really do that?" I asked.

"Definitely. Sheridan is ruthless. After Geronimo broke out recently, it became a real possibility. Crook chased him down into the Sierra Madre. Thank God Crook convinced him and his followers to come back. But if Geronimo does it again, it's over for the Chiricahuas. He'll bring ruin to his people."

"But Manolete wouldn't?" mother said.

"He's a lot smarter than that drunken degenerate. And Manolete cares about his people. Geronimo cares only about himself. Most of his people despise him. That's why Crook had no trouble getting Apache scouts to help track him in Mexico. They won't offer to hunt down Manolete."

"So you're sure he won't do what Geronimo did?" mother asked.

"Manolete knows what will happen if he does. And even Crook won't be able to stop it. Sheridan will get his way."

"He's the head of the army now?"

"And a sad day it was when he was given the command. He's the one who coined the phrase that's become so popular out here—that the only good Indians he ever saw were dead."

"That disgusts me," mother said.

"Sheridan and Crook were friends once, classmates at West Point. They fell out during the War. Sheridan stole the credit for Crook's success in the Shenandoah. Crook has never forgiven him. It's the only grudge I've ever known Crook to hold. He looks on Sheridan like a suppurating wound. He'll take that feeling to his grave."

All of us sat in silence for a while.

"There's one thing I don't understand," mother said after several minutes. "If what you say about Manolete is correct, then why do you still seem worried?"

"Two reasons. The first is the young bucks who fled with him. They're looking for action, as young men will. They might leave the Mexican mountains without him and terrorize this land. And they'll be completely out of control."

Silence followed again. Finally I said, "Mac . . . ?"

"Yes?"

"You said there were two reasons."

He took a long deep breath and let it out slowly. It was not a sigh but something more ominous.

"The second reason is that I might be completely and absolutely wrong. At this very moment, he might be planning the most terrible atrocities ever to scar Apacheria."

"But you know him," I said, trying to argue him out of it.

"No, sweetheart. No white man ever truly knows the mind of Manolete."

We listened to the owl and to the rustling of the cottonwoods for a while, and then mother said she was going to make some tea.

I liked being alone with Mac. That night I realized for the first time that before him I had never in my life been completely alone and had a private conversation with a man. This could not have been an accident on mother's part. Nor could her leaving us alone at that moment have been a simple happenstance. It was her gift to me, and to Mac. Not until I had girls of my own did I comprehend that she had given Mac—deliberately—a sacred trust.

"Mac, do you ask God for favors?"

He laughed softly. "Every soldier does. There are no atheists in the Arizona Territory."

"Does God answer you?"

"Every time."

"Stop teasing me," I said with a giggle.

"I'm not."

"He always gives you what you want?"

"I didn't say that."

"But you said—."

Apacheria

"Sometimes He answers no."

"Oh, that's not fair! That's not what I asked."

He tousled my hair. "Why are you asking me this?"

"Can I tell you a secret?"

"If you'd like to."

"I prayed at Mass that you'd stay here. I asked God to convince you, even if you didn't want to. Was it bad? I mean to try to force you."

"It's never bad to talk with God. And never wrong to ask for what you want."

"But I tried to get Him to—."

"God is usually pretty clever at separating the good from the not so good. He'll figure it out."

I reached out for his right hand. "I'm sorry."

"Don't be. No need. Now can I tell you a secret?"

That stunned me. I could not believe that this man, this Indian fighter, my hero . . . could not imagine that he would tell a little girl a secret.

"Yes," I whispered.

"Sometimes God answers prayers we never even make. And those are the grandest gifts of all."

I smiled, and we just sat there in silence and enjoyed the night.

After a while, he said, "Katy . . ."

I looked up at him.

"You don't have to hold my hand so tight."

I quickly released it.

"I didn't say let it go." He took mine back gently in his callused fingers. "There's just no need for a death grip. I won't slip away."

I hesitated for a moment, and then said, "Can I tell you another secret?"

"This is turning out to be a special night."

"When I was little, I used to ask God for a brother or sister."

"When you were little?" he said with a gentle laugh. "I see.

But not anymore?"

"I didn't really want them. But I knew to get them I had to have a father first."

"Ah. So you tried to fox God. Catch Him unawares."

I hesitated. "That sounds silly now."

"Well, now that you're older and wiser, many things will." His voice was so tender and understanding I never wanted this night to end.

"One more secret?" I asked.

"As many as you like."

"I'm glad God answered me with a no. It was what I wanted more than anything in the world, but now I'm glad He said no."

Mac was one of those rare adults who always responded to what a child said, no matter how trivial it might have seemed to him. But this time he did not. He just stared at me and rubbed his rough thumb softly over the back of my hand. Then he looked away.

I snuggled up closer to him, and we sat there in silence as the owl hooted in the distance. We were quiet for what seemed like years. Mac cleared his throat once but never spoke. I was surprised to feel a raindrop hit my fingers resting atop his hand on his leg. I looked up. The sky was clear. I turned to him and saw that his cheek was wet.

Tension suddenly rippled through him. Our owl's hoots sounded odd, a bit sharper and coming in quick succession. I had never heard anything like that before.

"Let's go in," Mac said. "Time for a cup of tea."

Later there was a strange ending to the day. I slept restlessly. I woke up in the middle of the night and saw the room drenched in moonlight. Mother was sound asleep beside me.

Outside I heard the crunching of footsteps. I got up and peered out the window. Mac was walking toward the corral. Reba was already waiting for him with her head and neck extended over the rail. He stroked her forehead and then he pressed his face against hers. She sniffed and nuzzled her master, and he seemed to draw the peace of Heaven from her touch. Then he laid his arms across the rail and lowered his forehead on them and just rested there. Whether pain or sorrow or joy or longing filled him I could not say. Adult passions were at that time just beginning to press against the edge of my comprehension.

Meanwhile, Reba stood over him like a sentinel, her large wise eyes scanning the dark for predators.

14

Clete Lomaddis baffled me. I could never understand why he lived in our town. Almost no one liked him, and those who did were not worth liking either. That he was a criminal of some sort I did not doubt. Yet my revulsion, and probably that of most people, had little to do with suspicions of wrongdoing. He was simply a hugely unlikable man. It was as if he were cursed by a perverse demon to wander the earth to make people recoil. Why could he not just leave?

As always, mother had the answer, though I was not sure I fully understood it. She said he lived in our town out of vengeance. He would never be liked, she said, anywhere. So he shoved it in people's faces every day, and in that twisted way derived sustenance from a blighted life. An existence maintained by revenge. Like feeding on carrion. It was horrifying to me and insane. Yet I never doubted mother's insights into people's souls. Most frightening to me was the thought that only Satan himself could have concocted such a scheme. Ever after, when I spied Lomaddis, I saw a soldier in the army of the dead.

So I was shocked that morning when I felt sorry for him. I was sitting on the edge of the boardwalk outside our merc and trying to whittle a horse's head. I was using a carving by Pino as a model. He had given me a small folding knife that he said his father had given him. It looked as old as Pino, and I was reluctant to take it. But he had pressed it into my hand with that

great grin. He found me a chunk of soft pine, and I went to work. What I produced looked less like Pegasus than like a misshapen dog with a tumor on his neck.

Lomaddis came racing down the street. Anger and fear distorted his features into an object of pity. At least to me. Of course, the swollen purple bruises Mac had given him did not help matters.

He pulled up in front of the sheriff's office and hurried inside.

That was too much for me. I folded my knife and looped the leather lanyard around my neck and raced down the street.

Jim was always very tolerant of me. He would shoo me away only if there were the threat of bad language or something even more inappropriate for an eleven-year-old girl. He glanced at me as I came into his office, and then turned back to Lomaddis, who was ranting away.

From what I could gather, Lomaddis had taken possession of Mr. Devlin's place a few days ago, and last night some Apaches had struck. They stole some of Clete's horses and hazed off most of his cattle.

"They could have killed me in my bed and the law is doing nothing!"

Jim slouched on the edge of his desk. He was his customary calm self. "Did you see them?"

"No one sees Apaches, for Christ's sake."

"Watch your language."

"There were unshod pony tracks everywhere."

"I've heard nothing from Colonel Hargrave about Indian sign."

I thought of the hoofprints I had spotted along the river.

"Those stupid soldiers couldn't find pigs in a sty."

I wanted to punch his face.

"I'll look into it."

Lomaddis seemed like he was about to burst, but I was certain I saw a smile in Jim's eyes.

"Not such a game now, is it, Clete?"

He glared at Jim and then rushed out the door like a gust of bad air.

I went over and sat next to Jim on the desk. For a long time he had been my only hero. Then Mac had come. Oddly enough, I liked Jim even more now than I ever had. I think I appreciated him better for what he was, instead of what I wanted him to be. So easy going and relaxed, he could ride out any storm. Some of the boys mocked him behind his back because he often went unarmed. I knew him better than they did. His confidence and strength conveyed more power than any hogleg. I had seen him face down drunken louts with nothing more than a stare. Jim's anger was rare, but the toughest men in town always gave way before it. I think mother and I were the only people who knew his tender side. I had always assumed that someday he would be my stepfather. I no longer wanted that. So it was strange that now I felt closer to him than ever.

"How are you, cowgirl?" he said with a smile and pushed back my cavalry hat and brushed some hair away from my eyes.

"More than fine."

I felt my face reddening when I realized that was a phrase I had picked up from Mac.

"Why are you blushing?"

I just shrugged.

He reached behind himself on the desk for the jar he kept there for just such emergencies.

"For medicinal purposes," he said and pulled out a peppermint stick and handed it to me.

"Thank you."

He gazed at me pleasantly.

"Clete was really terrified, wasn't he?" I said.

"It's not easy for him to realize those Apaches could have taken his life as easily as his horse."

"What will happen?"

Apacheria

"A few more people might sell their ranches. I think Mac was right about that. And I'll talk with Captain Colton and see if anyone has spotted any sign along the river."

Mac had quieted me before when I had been about to mention what I had seen. But I still felt uncomfortable about my silence.

"Where's your colonel today?"

My colonel? Why would he say that?

"I don't know."

"I'm glad he's staying with you and your mother. I can sleep better."

I smiled. I wanted to hug him for saying that. But I knew he was not as comfortable with hugs as Mac was.

"He's a heck of a brawler, your friend," Jim said. "Like all these Irishmen. But he's a rock, too. No cold wind could hit the back of your neck while he's behind you."

I touched Jim's left hand resting on his leg. "Thanks for being our friend."

"Some things are just ordained to be."

Then out of nowhere he seemed suddenly sad. He turned away from me.

"I suppose that's the word," he said. "Ordained. No matter how hard we pray, some things can't be changed."

I sat there watching him as he gazed at something I could not see.

Finally, he turned to me with a smile, but it was a hurting smile.

"Go play, Katy. Go groom Dollar or listen to the songbirds. Breathing the air of a jail too long isn't good for anyone."

I wandered out to the street. I felt aimless today. Jim had sent me off, Mac was not to be found, and mother was busy at the mercantile. I met three of my girlfriends on the street, and they invited me to come and bake pies with them. But what they would really do is discuss boys. All day. I wanted none of that. Yet with mother and Mac and Jim all preoccupied, I was

surprised how I could not stop thinking about Timmy.

When I had turned eleven, I celebrated like I never had before. It was the end of childhood, and I was as happy as a kitten in cream. Ten years of being a "little" girl were enough. Now I wondered why I had looked forward to it so.

It occurred to me now how much Timmy reminded me of Jim. Steady and quiet and determined. If Timmy were ten years older, every unmarried woman in town would be fluttering her eyelashes at him. Why had I not realized that until today? Of course, Mac was my storybook hero. The bold man in blue. Bigger than life. Bigger than any girl dare imagine. He was the center of a great painting in my mind, the horseman of my dreams. And he always spoke to me as if I were a woman, and then my insides would snap the traces and race along at a mad gallop.

Timmy was different. Thoughts of him steadied me back to an easy lope. I knew, for reasons I could not explain, that this was life as it should be. And I knew equally well that Timmy was mine for the asking. That scared me, too.

Mother's honor box was doing duty when I got to our store. I wandered to the back room. Mother was sitting at the table. She was wearing her white dress with pink roses, the one she had been wearing the day Mac rode in. Yet it was the expression on her face I remember most clearly now. It was a look I had never before seen, on her on anyone else, nor have I seen it again, on her or on anyone else.

A letter lay unfolded on the table in front of her. Her right hand was across her mouth, as though her fingers were holding back something that might escape. Her elbow was hard on the table and propping up her chin. It seemed to need it. I could see her face only from the side, but an impossible mixture of joy and uncertainty spread across it like a swirl of paints on an artist's palette. Bafflement, too, crinkled her forehead. But, above all, gratitude lit her eyes. The shattering gratitude the man born blind must have felt when Jesus extended his hand and gave him sight. It shone around mother like the corona of an angel's glow.

I just stood there helpless. She must have heard me come in, but she did not react. I shifted my weight a little, and without looking up she stretched out her left arm. Her right fingers still pressed hard against her lips. I hurried to her. She pulled me tight, but still she did not speak.

Mac's boots on the floorboards were unmistakable

"Well, this looks far too solemn for such a beautiful morning," he said in his easy way as he came through the doorway.

Mother turned toward him.

"What's wrong, Mary?"

"Nothing," she said in a raspy whisper.

She eased her hold on me, and I knew that was a signal. I stepped away.

She stood up and faced him. She looked embarrassed. "I opened your mail by mistake. I'm sorry."

"Mail?"

"From a bank in Tucson."

"Oh that. I didn't have an address, so I gave them yours. I hope you don't mind."

"Mind?" Now mother gave up trying to conceal her feelings any longer. She finally surrendered. "Oh, Redmond, how can you do this?"

"Do what?"

He seemed genuinely puzzled.

"The trust fund."

He smiled and walked over to me. He pulled off my hat and ruffled my hair vigorously. "How could I not?"

"But . . . ?"

"The Fireball can use it to go East to a good school. Hone her literary skills. Or stay here and use it as a dowry and rear a beautiful family."

"But it's so much," mother said. "Your whole life."

"Maggie is smiling. Besides, what else am I going to do with it? Bury it with me?"

"Don't say that."

"I don't need much. I'm a simple man. With simple needs."

Mother stared at him with a look of such longing that I felt I should not be watching. "No you're not. You're the most complex man I know."

He grinned at me and I squeezed him as hard as I could. Then he looked back at mother. "Don't let it get around."

She tightened her lips, as if fearful again that something was about to slip out.

"Have you heard about Lomaddis?" Mac asked her.

"Oh, to Hell with Lomaddis!"

I gaped at her in shock. I had never heard her use such language. This would be a memorable day in all sorts of ways.

She spun around toward the window, but I doubt she saw anything outside. Mac came over to her and laid a hand on her shoulder. She closed her eyes with obvious pleasure, and her whole body relaxed and went soft. Finally she whispered, "Please . . . ."

I had no idea why she said that, but Mac apparently understood and let his hand fall away.

"Tell us about Lomaddis," she said.

Us. She had directed Mac away from her toward the both of us again. I could not comprehend that.

"Apparently he had some visitors last night. He said Apaches ran off some of his stock."

Mother turned away from the window and looked at Mac. "He said?"

"Well, he didn't see them."

"But there were prints of unshod ponies," I said.

"And how do you know that?" Mac asked.

"I heard Lomaddis tell Sheriff Blaine. Tracks like—." I stopped.

"Like the ones we saw along the river?"

"*You* saw?" mother said. "Why didn't you mention it?"

Apacheria

"Because it isn't important," Mac said.

"That doesn't make sense," mother went on. "Are you protecting those Indians?"

Even from the back room, we could hear the commotion outside.

Mac turned and went out the door. We were close behind.

I can still remember the feel of that morning, fresh and cool and the birds singing. A buckboard was parked in the middle of the street and people were gathering around. The sheriff looked grim.

"Oh my God," mother said when we got up to the wagon.

Mr. Devlin lay inside, riddled with arrows beyond counting.

"I found him on the road," Scabby said.

"Oh Lord. Was he still alive, Norbert?" mother asked.

"Barely. He died on the way in."

"Why did they have to do this?" mother said. "He was leaving anyway. He was riding out."

"Because they're not men!" Lomaddis shouted. "They're bucks!"

"Shut up," Jim said, and Lomaddis got quiet.

I touched Mac's sleeve and he looked down at me.

"Why are the arrows just stumps?"

"Because they shot him slowly so he'd die slowly. It's the Apache way. He rolled around in agony and the shafts snapped off. I've seen it before." He looked back at Mr. Devlin. "Never thought I'd see it again."

"I need a volunteer to go to the fort," Jim said.

"I will," Lomaddis answered.

Jim turned to Scabby. "Norbert?"

"I'll go," he said.

Lomaddis looked insulted.

"Get the undertaker," Jim said to no one in particular. "And the padre."

15

Fear swept across our town like a cold rain. The lovely days of early summer might as well not have been happening. It was as if an icy wet rag had been wrapped around people's faces and they were unable to breathe, or simply afraid to.

Sheriff Blaine verified the pony tracks at Lomaddis's place. When word got around, three more ranchers put their spreads for sale, and Clete snatched them up. Some townspeople speculated that he had faked the whole thing just for that purpose. I knew they were wrong. He might be profiting from the crisis, but his fear had been real.

Every bit as real as everyone else's. Yet I had no fear. How could I? After all, I had mother. Regardless of what she might feel deep down, bending to fear was not part of her way of living. Yielding would have been incomprehensible to her. All of my girlfriends had fine parents, but years later my friends told me how much they had admired mother that summer. Tall and straight as an unchoppable tree, one of them had said. Able to see what others could not, another had offered, and as brave as an Apache buck.

And yet to herself, mother seemed entirely ordinary. She never understood why others turned to her for guidance and looked to her for strength. I think this bafflement was the biggest reason my friends admired her so.

Apacheria

But mother was not the only reason to be unafraid. Jim Blaine was there as well. The greater the crisis the calmer Jim became. He was a bit warier now, that was true, and certainly more alert. But he had a steadying hand that reassured all who came within his reach. Jim was no asset to a dinner party, but to a town in fear he was a gift from Heaven.

And then there was Mac. The comfort I drew from him was of a different order entirely. His experience of good and evil had been so vast that it had imbued him with a confidence and a serenity a monk could envy. To others, he was just a horse soldier, battle-scarred perhaps, but no more than that. To me, he was worlds beyond. When he had first ridden in, I had been impressed by his bearing, how he sat a horse, just the cover of the book. Now such things were all in the past. So many more chapters filled that volume. That he was an educated man I never doubted. In the evenings in front of the fire, he had begun reading *The Aeneid* to me. Soon I felt as if Virgil himself were speaking to me from across the ages. Occasionally Mac would teach me small Latin phrases from the poem. Where he had been schooled, other than West Point, I did not know. He never spoke of his parents, and I had no idea if they were still living. Nor did he mention any siblings, though an Irish only child seemed a contradiction of the laws of nature. It was as if his personal life were beyond a hill in a hidden valley that I might someday be allowed to enter, but not yet.

There was another Mac, too, far different from the savorer of Virgilian verses. This was the student of human strife. He seemed to know every detail of every battle since man first leaped into a saddle. I was so grateful he did not believe it inappropriate for a girl to hear these tales. One evening was especially memorable. That was the night I felt the terror of the Battle of the Sabis.

We were having an early summer rain and the wind was lashing the water against the windows. Mother had excused me from the dishes, and I was curled up with Mac on the sofa in

front of the fire. I was cozy in my nightdress and robe. Yet in an instant it was a warm day and I was marching with Caesar in the land of the Nervii, the most warlike and savage of the Belgic tribes.

Caesar was relying on his famous luck and on his speed — his *celeritas* — which had become the byword of his campaigns. Because of inadequate scouting along the Sabis River — "No scouting at all," Mac said — the Nervii swooped down upon his legions.

With the voice of a poet, Mac regaled me with the plight of the Romans. The desperation, the fear, the chaos. Caesar on horseback rushing to every part of the buckling line to bolster his men. Then the legionaries being attacked from opposite sides and having to form a pair of lines back to back and counterattacking in two directions at once. Finally the rally, the discipline, the staggering valor. And then the crushing of the Nervii in one of the greatest feats of arms in the history of civilized man.

When Mac was finished, I realized I was panting and my mouth was sand. Mother, too, had been swept up. She had forgotten the dishes and stood staring at Mac with parted lips behind the easy chair, her fingers digging into the cushion.

"Shakespeare wrote that the day the traitors killed Caesar, he was wearing a robe he had first worn the night he had beaten the Nervii." Mac smiled. "Perhaps that was just Shakespeare. But if it was true, it was fitting."

I slid over to Mac and snuggled up against him. I could not figure out if he were a soldier who was also a man of letters, or a poet and scholar who happened to lead men on horseback into battle. For months I struggled with that puzzle, until eventually it faded away and was forgotten. Years later I recalled it, and I knew that the reason the mystery had vanished was not that it had ever been solved. Rather, to the little girl, and to the woman she became, it was a mystery that mattered no longer. And then with a smile I realized that it had never really mattered at all.

Apacheria

After Mass on Sunday and breakfast at the Paradise, mother and Mac and I were walking past the gun store when Mr. Shapiro waved us over. He was never open for business on Sunday, out of deference to us Christians. His Sabbath was over, though, so he was usually in his shop and working harder than any three men.

We went inside. He was already behind the counter and reaching underneath it. I could hear Mrs. Shapiro clattering around in the back somewhere.

"For you, colonel," he said and placed a holster on top of the glass case.

It was a tribute to the leather maker's art. Not the usual sloppy belt scabbard that satisfied the cowboys, this was a sleek shoulder holster. The rich russet leather had been border tooled with a skill that came only from years' worth of squinting over the workbench.

Stunned, Mac picked it up and looked at Mr. Shapiro.

"Thank you, sir. What's the occasion?"

"You speak for zose too veak to speak for zemselves. You speak vit honor vhen it is easy not to speak at all."

Mac smiled.

"You are Irish, ja?"

"Yes."

Now Mr. Shapiro smiled. "Ve can haf a cup of coffee zometime and discuss za ghettos ve haf known."

Mac slipped the holster over his left shoulder. "Perfect fit."

"Zat old army holster you haf. Oy! Za flap—I call zat za vidowmaker."

Mac laughed.

"Zis vay it's easy to use your saber or carbine."

Mac shook Mr. Shapiro's hand. "Thank you again."

Mac was quiet all the way home. Mother sat beside him on the buckboard, and I bounced around in the back. Not a word

passed between them.

I was startled to see the sheriff's horse hitched in front of our place. We went in and the house smelled like coffee. Jim was already pouring.

"I hope you don't mind that I started a pot."

"You're always welcome here, Jim," mother said, removing her hat. "What's wrong?"

We all sat at the table together.

"Scabby let me down," Jim said to Mac. "He never got back to me after I sent him to the fort."

"That's the problem with amateurs," Mac said. "You get what you pay for."

"If you have the time, will you ride out there with me today? You have entrée that no one else does."

"Katy, change your clothes and saddle up," Mac said.

I could not believe my good fortune. I ran to the bedroom.

"I want her with me," I heard Mac say to mother from the other room. "She's writing all this in her diary. I want her to see and hear as much as she can. Don't worry. She's safe."

"I know," mother said. "I'm not worried."

When I had changed, I grabbed my cavalry hat and raced back out of the bedroom.

"Tack up Reba, too," Mac told me.

Then he went in to change, and we were on the road in minutes.

Mac wore his new holster over a dark blue engineer's shirt. The nickel and ivory Colt looked more at home in the reddish brown leather than it had in the army holster. I had asked him once about the nickel. I said I thought it seemed too fancy for a soldier.

"So did I," he said. "Until I'd ridden and slept in a winter rain for three days and nights."

"Didn't you have a tent to sleep in?"

He laughed. "Rarely. Believe me, Fireball, the Apaches aren't a soldier's greatest enemy. Rust is."

Apacheria

   The three of us rode out across the grassland, lush now from those winter rains that had so tormented Mac and his men. Amidst the grasses, century plants threw up their stalks to bloom the instant before they died. Easterners were often repelled by agaves, with their harsh leaves and their eerie race toward blossoming and death. To me they were one of nature's great glories, as emblematic of this land as the saguaro was symbolic of the desert not far away.
   We could see a long way off. I could hardly wait to get to the fort. The soldiers and the army mounts and maybe even Colonel Hargrave bowing again and kissing my hand. But it was not to be. We never made it to Huachuca that day.
   I was the first to spot the smoke. Just a wisp of black barely visible to the southwest.
   "Mac," I said, pointing.
   It made no sense, because there was nothing out here to burn, other than the grass itself. And it was too green for that now.
   "Let's check it," Jim said, and the three of us loped off.
   The smoke was thicker than it had seemed from a distance. As we got closer, the wind changed and we began smelling it, too. A strong scent hit me. It seemed like burnt pork, as if a big hog haunch on a spit had been thrown over a mesquite fire and forgotten about. It puzzled me why anyone would be camping out here, when towns were so close by.
   I turned to Mac as we rode on. The look on his face was one I had never seen before, on him or anyone else. No painter could have captured it. Though I can see it as clearly now as if it were still before me, I can scarcely describe it. A strange mixture of anger and sorrow and loathing distorted his features into an impossible expression. And it frightened me, even though I knew I could never be frightened of Mac. Most of all, it saddened me. His eyes were those of someone escorted by a demon to the netherworld and allowed to peer over the edge of the abyss.

A dark hulk burned in front of us. At first I was not sure what I was seeing. When we got closer, I realized it was a wagon, and the smoke made me start coughing. We circled it and got upwind. Three arrow-riddled bodies lay some distance from the wagon. The burnt pork smell was overwhelming, with a toasty sweetness that for a moment seemed almost pleasant, but in another instant it soured my stomach. I have never eaten pork again.

The wagon was just smoldering now, and lashed to a rear wheel was what looked like a black stickman. It had once been a human being.

Mac dismounted, and Jim and I did, too. Mac walked over to the wagon. The muscles in his jaw looked like knotted ropes. I went up next to him. He made no attempt to shield me from the horror.

"Who are they?" Mac asked Jim.

"The three on the ground are part of the posse that rode out the day you came to town." He looked at the grotesque figure on the wheel. "That lump of charcoal—I think it's Scabby."

"Oh, God," I said.

"Do you have your knife, Katy?" Mac asked.

I dug out the little folder Pino had given me. Mac took it and cut the scorched thongs off Scabby's wrists and laid him gently down.

I turned away.

"God have mercy on us," Jim said, and even he seemed frightened now. "Manolete is here."

We rode back. Jim went on alone—he was that brave. He rode to all the outlying ranches to warn as many people as he could. Mac took me into town to mother.

The death of Scabby hit mother hard. She alone of those I knew had never called him by the cruel nickname we had used without thought. She had seen beyond the superficial. That

evening she went to her room and prayed the rosary. I knew it was for Norbert.

The requiem Mass was wrenching. The weather did not help. A gorgeous day seemed to mock the agony of the mourners. I wished that God would have allowed the heavens to weep, but He did not.

I had never been to a funeral, other than that of the little Vogt boy who had died of scarlet fever. Though Norbert had been only twenty-three, his parents were elderly, and this just shattered them. They sat slumped in the first pew like collapsed husks.

Lomaddis was there, too, and the menacing figure of Skeels, and all the other toughs Norbert had clung to in order to feel tough himself. It was all pointless now.

Afterward, the Willoughbys had arranged for a breakfast at the hotel for everyone at the funeral. I knew mother did not want to attend, but when poor Mrs. Willoughby asked her to sit beside her, there was no chance mother would refuse.

I was relieved when it was over. I had felt like I was suffocating in the crowded dining room. It was a sweet release to get out onto the street and breathe the summer air.

Mac had been right—soldiers were popular again. People clustered around him for advice. Like most wise words, they were just common sense. Yet people seemed to draw comfort from the fact that they came from a man who had worn the blue. Never go unarmed, travel only in groups, stay close to the ranch house as much as possible, leave the occasional stray to the coyotes.

Mother needed no prompting. She now wore her Schofield revolver on her right hip as nonchalantly as if she were a stagecoach guard. She favored the Wells Fargo hogleg with the shortened barrel. And it was not there just to say howdy do. I was certain she could shoot better than half the men in town and at least as well as most.

The afternoon of the funeral, Mac rode out to the fort. He

changed his clothes following Mass, and when I saw him getting ready to ride, I grabbed my cavalry hat. He shook his head. "Not today," he said, and rode out alone. I was disappointed, but I did not whine about it.

So strange is a young girl's mind that when Mac got back, all I wanted to hear about was how Colonel Hargrave was getting along with his troopers. But Mac said nothing about that or about anything else.

Jim stopped by for a cup of coffee on his way to checking the farthest ranches. He told us that some of the townsmen had let out an Indian hunting contract to Skeels and Lomaddis and their hangers-on.

"Skeels stipulated that all Apache scalps were his," Jim said. "The scalphunter returns. Just what I need. And he won't be moving on either. He's bought up those ranches for a handful of beads. Now he can become a pillar of the community."

"Private armies," Mac said, shaking his head. "As controllable as rabid dogs."

"Well, at least they *are* an army," Jim said. "Not like that useless regiment at Huachuca."

Mother tensed. I glanced at Mac. His eyes looked like frozen glass. I noticed his knuckles were white around the coffee cup. But he remained silent.

Jim was frazzled. I was sure that was why he had said that.

"Is that what the fort is for?" Jim said. "So the soldier boys can trot their horses around the parade ground? Do we—?"

"Jim . . ." mother said, laying a hand on his sleeve.

"No, he's right," Mac said. "Soldiers recline on velvet cushions. Didn't you know that? But their lives will be even sweeter when they hear Sheriff Blaine's charming philosophical reflections. It isn't enough that these smiling boys come out here looking for adventure and end up festering like a boil on the ass end of Hell. Not enough that their life is so deadly boring that we're breeding a race of drunks and degenerate gamblers. That their rations are slop you wouldn't throw to a dog in the street. That they've never even been taught how to hold a saber. Or

Apacheria

been allowed to fire more than five rounds from their pistols—ever—because ammunition is expensive, don't you know? That they're constantly goaded by the whites into finishing off the rest of the Indians, as if we haven't already finished them off by killing their souls. Or that when we bring murdering Apaches to justice, the do-gooders in tweeds from the East condemn us as butchers and worse. Drooling barbarians ignorant of the delicate nuances of Apache culture. But maybe that's because we're too busy cradling the corpses of slaughtered mothers. And babies with crushed skulls whose brains are falling out onto our boots. And all for fame and glory and thirteen dollars a month. Isn't that so, Blaine? And for that we have the sublime pleasure of being told by you—you—that our life is actually a slice of Paradise. Lectured to by a small-town sheriff whose biggest challenge is sidestepping the vomit of the local drunks." Mac stood up. "So on behalf of the regiment allow me to thank you. Before today we just had half-mad whites and bleeding heart fools to deal with. But just when we believed we'd reached the pinnacle of delight"—he swept his hand toward Jim as if he were introducing a celebrity—"we're honored to be instructed by *you*."

Mac turned away and strode across the room and out the door.

I looked at Jim. He could not have been more stunned than if he had been struck by lightning.

"Excuse me, Mary," he said and picked up his hat and walked outside.

I went to the window. Jim and Mac were speaking quietly. I hurried to the door.

"Katy—stay inside."

I ran back to the window.

"Come away from there," mother said. "Start the dishes."

I went over to the sink, but I had barely begun when I heard a horse lope off.

"I'll finish," mother said.

William Altimari

I hurried back to the window. Jim was gone, and Mac was walking away. I knew where he was going. To Reba—to the scent and quiet and solace of his queen.

16

No longer did it seem to be early summer. The lovely weather was taunting us, because now everyone's spirit was darkening like mid-day in mid-July when the summer monsoons came rumbling up from Mexico. The air itself tensed with a taut half-calm that foretold the imminent storm. And rushing in now was a torrent far more fierce than rain.

I was helping mother load up some shelves in our mercantile when a cavalry office strode in. He was maybe forty-five, not as handsome as Captain Colton — who on earth was? — but he had the horse soldier's self-assurance. It trailed off him, that seeming arrogance that infantrymen found so annoying but which to me was nothing less than God-like.

"Good morning, major," mother said. "How may I help you?"

"Ma'am," he said, removing his hat. "Major Conahan. I was told I might find Colonel McGregor here."

"You might," she answered but said nothing else.

I smiled. She was as imposing as any man, even a cavalryman.

The major grinned. "The colonel always knew how to pick his sentries. Will you convey a message?"

"I will."

"Tell him the Gray Fox is here to see him."

She looked at me. "Katy."

I hurried to the back room where Mac and Jim were seated at the table and looking over a map. I told Mac what the major had said.

"The earth has shaken," Mac said to Jim, and then he turned to me. "Get your hat, Fireball."

We went back into the store.

"Good to see you, Gene," Mac said.

The major pulled off his gauntlet and shook Mac's hand. "You're looking fine sir."

"I'm being well cared for."

The major glanced at mother. She was smiling at Mac with feelings that needed no deciphering.

"I see," the major said.

"Where is he?"

"The hotel."

"Let's go."

I grabbed my hat from the counter.

"This is private, sir," the major said.

Mac took his hat from a hanger on the back wall. "My aide goes with me everywhere."

Mac asked no questions as we crossed the street to the Paradise. Three lean cavalry horses and a mule were hitched out front.

The Paradise had one special suite for newlyweds or for anyone else who wanted something more than four bare walls and a hard bed. We went inside without knocking.

A table had been set up in the small sitting room. A short man wearing a canvas hunting jacket was seated in the middle on the other side. He looked like a civilian. A cork sun helmet lay at one edge of the table. Two officers flanked him, and all were studying a map much bigger than the one Mac and Jim had.

"Good morning, colonel," the man in the middle said with barely a glance up as he made notations on the map.

"General," Mac said, removing his hat.

I pulled off mine.

Apacheria

"All right," the general said to his officers, and they blotted the inked notations and rolled up the map. He looked at Mac and me. "Be seated."

Mac placed two chairs before the desk and we sat.

"And this officer?" the general said, looking at me with eyes as sharp as arrowheads.

"Lieutenant Malone, my aide-de-camp."

"I see." I think his gaze softened a bit and he turned to Mac. "You've always had a fine eye for officer material."

"Yes, sir."

The general sported the most outrageous beard I had ever seen. It shot out left and right from his jaw in two giant wiry triangles. His gray hair was cut short, but the beard made his head seem enormous. He reminded me of an engraving I had once seen of a Prussian army officer.

He folded his hands on the table. "Shall we speak of Manolete?"

No preliminaries. No small talk. I was already getting excited to know this man.

"Certainly, sir."

The general leaned over to Major Conahan and whispered something to him. The major left immediately.

"I'm on my way to Huachuca to talk with Hargrave, but I want an informal assessment from you first. From a field officer with more experience."

"Yes, sir."

"I'm not sanguine about what I've been hearing. And don't feed me from the end of a pin."

Mac began a narrative of all that had occurred since he had arrived. His ability to recall detail was extraordinary, and he also provided excellent little portraits of everyone involved.

The general was equally impressive but in a different way. He sat back relaxed in his chair, but a searing concentration focused on Mac's every word.

As Mac was finishing, Major Conahan returned with a tray

and set it on the table. He poured me a glass of lemonade from a pitcher and a cup of coffee from a blue pot for Mac.

"All right," the general said. "Those are the facts. Now you know what I want."

Mac took a sip of his coffee. "What I'm about to tell you, sir, I've shared with no one except Colonel Hargrave two days ago."

"Proceed."

"General, I believe that Manolete perpetrated nothing of what I've described to you."

I think I was actually open-mouthed as I stared at Mac. I looked back at the general. He seemed not surprised at all, though his officers were stunned.

"Explain," the general said, clearly for their benefit rather than his own.

"First, the unshod ponies. This is the eighties, not the sixties. I'll wager Manolete hasn't ridden an unshod horse in a decade or more. Even if it was his own, let alone a stolen one."

"And the tracks?" Major Conahan said.

"Somebody pulled the shoes."

"But wouldn't that have been obvious?"

"To a tracker," Mac said. "To me. The edges of the prints would have been sharper than usual. Even the nail holes might have been visible if the ground was soft enough. But the sheriff is no Al Sieber. He saw what he expected to see."

Mac went back to his coffee.

"Continue, colonel," the general said.

"Old man Devlin—riddled with arrows? For God's sake, Manolete probably doesn't even own a bow. He and his men have Springfields and Winchesters. Don't misunderstand. Manolete is capable of any atrocity. But capability isn't the same as actuality."

"What about this Norbert wretch?" Conahan said. "Tired to a wagon and torched."

"White men did it."

"How do you know that?" the general said.

Apacheria

Mac pulled from his watch pocket what looked like two black strings. "I cut these thongs from Norbert, sir." He laid them on the table.

The general picked one up.

"Look at the hitch, sir. It's a bowline. No Apache would tie a bowline."

"Maybe by accident," Conahan said.

Mac took the other one and tossed it to him. "Twice?" He looked back at the general. "It's designed to hitch a wet line so it won't slip. It's a sailor's knot."

"Oh!" I shouted, and then caught myself.

"Yes, lieutenant?" the general said.

"Lomaddis was a sailor sir," I said.

The general looked at Mac.

"Manolete's outbreak is like a vein of Mexican silver, sir. Ranches are being bought up at a fraction of their values. A fortune is being made here."

"I see," the general said. "And is this Lomaddis capable of such a thing?"

"Yes, but there's a darker mind at work here. I believe it's Alejandro Skeels. The scalphunter. Lieutenant Malone said Lomaddis was genuinely terrified when he thought Apaches had hazed off his horses. I believe her. Skeels did it without telling Lomaddis at first so he could scare everyone. Fire the first shot to stampede the herd."

"And they sacrificed Norbert Willoughby and the other three?" Conahan asked.

"Those were nothing to them," Mac said.

The general took a deep breath and let it out slowly. "One thing puzzles me. Why didn't you share this with the sheriff?"

"Because I'm not certain, sir. I could be wrong. Maybe I'm just being too clever. I'd rather the sheriff and everyone else be prepared for the worst from Manolete and not let their guard down."

The general smiled. "You've always been reckless with your

own life, Red, and cautious with everyone else's."

"Well, sir that's better than the other way around."

"Indeed. And Colonel Hargrave?"

"Sir?"

"Can he handle this crisis?"

"He's a fine officer, sir."

"I know that. But some were doubtful about giving him a field command."

"Then they're fools, sir."

The general's eyes were suddenly as cold as flint. "*I* was doubtful."

"Well, sir, I believe the general has become important enough in this man's army to be allowed the privilege of changing his mind."

The other three officers looked uncomfortable.

"Do you?" the general said.

"Yes, sir."

"I *am* that important, make no mistake, colonel."

Mac remained silent.

"I've heard that morale is very high at Huachuca."

"I have no knowledge of that, sir."

"Supposedly the troops are eating better than a general's dog robbers."

"Colonel Hargrave might be supplementing the usual garbage, sir. He has considerable inherited wealth."

"Yes. I knew his father. A hard man. Bit of a martinet."

"Yes, sir."

"I've also heard the incredible story that he's been breaking regulations by gambling with his men in their barracks. Supposedly they've even given him a nickname—Jack o' Clubs."

Mac smiled but said nothing.

"*You* I'd have expected that of, but Jack Hargrave?"

"Life *is* strange, isn't it, sir?"

The general took Mac's measure for a few moments.

"I don't believe I've seen you in civilian clothes before, colonel. Can't say I favor it."

Apacheria

"After army blue, sir, everything is a step down."

"Do you have plans?"

"Tentative, sir."

"Do they involve Arizona?"

I held my breath.

"They do, sir."

The general looked away toward the window. "Arizona is a strange drug. Cruel and intoxicating at the same time. When they first sent me here in the seventies, I considered it a slap. And now...."

"You've made history here, sir."

"Well," he said with a sigh, "I don't know if I've made it, but I've certainly changed it."

We all sat in silence for a spell.

"I always need scouts," the general said, turning back to Mac.

"Yes, sir."

"And I don't mean saddle bums who couldn't find a buffalo trail in a mud wallow. I mean someone like you."

"Thank you, sir."

"How are you fixed?"

Mac looked at me and winked. "Sir, I'm wealthy beyond the dreams of avarice."

A surprisingly warm smile softened the general's face. "I don't mean that kind of wealth."

"Sir, Sieber and I would make a poor marriage. Dutchmen rub my feathers the wrong way."

"Forget Sieber. Working for me—on an ad hoc basis. As needed."

"General, I'm always privileged to serve you. But if my first scout is riding down into the Sierra Madre to find Manolete, you need another man."

The general leaned forward and folded his hands in front of him. "Why?"

"I don't care how many *rurales* and *federales* he kills. Corrupt

thugs in The Land of Corruption."

"And if he comes here?"

"If I see him near those I care about, I'll cut him down before he can breathe."

The general straightened up. "I might call on you — for other things. I don't see you lolling in a rocking chair."

Mac smiled. "Only if it has a saddle, sir."

"I suppose we're finished here."

"General," I said quickly before Mac could get up.

"Yes?"

Looking into the general's eyes was like gazing into a great book. Arrayed before me and extending to invisibility was page after page of knowledge and wisdom compiled at a cost I could only dimly comprehend. For one precious and staggering instant, I was staring down the endless corridors of history.

"May I have your signature on a piece of paper, sir? To save? As a memento for my diary?"

He dipped his pen into the ink bottle and wrote on a small slip of notepaper. He blotted it and handed it to me.

George Crook
Brig. Gen. USArmy

"Thank you, sir."

He smiled at me and turned to Mac. "You're looking very well, Red."

"I'm more than fine, sir."

The general glanced at me. "I can see that."

He stood up and Mac did likewise and they shook hands.

"Please give my best to Bourke, sir. It's been many a scout since we dipped into the slumgullion together."

"I believe he's considering writing a book about his years out here. You'll probably be in it. He has dozens of volumes of diaries."

"He's the man to do it, sir. He has the flair."

"A braver man never wore a saber. I suppose I should tell him that someday. Tell him before I drop dead from stress."

"He'd appreciate that, sir."

"He's not too happy these days. Thinks I don't appreciate him. Too stingy with praise and promotions."

"I understand that, sir."

That caught the general off guard. His gaze hardened. "You understand it about him? Or you understand it about it me?"

Mac returned the hard gaze. "Yes, sir."

The general glared at him. "Did I ever tell you what I overheard a junior officer in your regiment say years ago? He said that McGregor is an impossible man to hate, but a difficult man to like."

A smile seeped into Mac's eyes. "General, I'd argue if I could."

"Good day to you both."

We were at the door when the general called out, "Colonel!"

We turned around together.

"Jack o' Clubs?" the general said, and for the first and only time that day I heard his hearty laugh. "That has you all over it."

"Well, sir—."

"Yes, I know, I know," he said, still laughing. "You'd argue if you could."

17

Mother always said that God had created the Sabbath not for homage to Himself, but as His reward to man. On a balmy Sunday morning after Mass, who could believe otherwise? I surely could not, because this would turn out to be one of the most memorable days of my life.

Mac was currying Reba in the shadow of a cottonwood near the corral. She was haltered and tied to the top rail as he tended her lovingly.

I sat in the shade on an upended bucket and watched. Renegades and killers were miles from my mind. Not until many years later would I realize that one of the purest joys of childhood was this wondrous shortness of perspective. Tomorrow was a hazy abstraction, and next week was barely a dream.

"Mac?"

"Mmmm?" He set down the curry and reached for the stiff brush.

"Why do they issue dull sabers to the troopers?"

Though he was turned almost all the way around, I could just make out the corner of his face and see him smiling to himself.

"Because there's a special department in the army to deal with these matters." He ran the brush over Reba and she began to glow with a beautiful copper sheen. "Not everybody can

Apacheria

belong to it. The qualifications are high. The most important is that you have to have fallen on your head at least half a dozen times. When the army runs out of those types, they make a sweep of the asylums."

I started laughing, and he turned around and tossed me the brush.

He came over and sat down Indian style on the ground in front of me.

"We call this agglomeration of the twisted and the mad The Ordnance Department."

"Who are they?"

"They design and issue uniforms and equipment. A gaggle of selected morons who don't understand how cold it gets on the northern plains, so the soldiers up there freeze and lose body parts. But down here the churn heads make sure we have plenty of wool to keep us cozy in the desert."

"Stop teasing me."

"I'm serious, sweetheart. These are the halt and the lame who issue us single shot rifles, while the Sioux and the Cheyenne have repeaters and can wipe out Custer's men like crippled grouse."

"What about the sabers?"

"Oh, that doesn't matter anymore. The saber is obsolete."

Mac must have seen the disillusionment in my eyes.

"Fireball, if you're close enough to an Indian to run him through with a saber, you're too close to survive the encounter."

"But *you* carry a saber."

"It's the symbol of the cavalry. I'll never be without it. But saber exercises are fading away."

"That doesn't seem right."

"Much of life isn't. But that's the way of the world."

His gentle smile had such understanding and compassion. I just loved him for it.

"But I'll bet *your* men know how to use a saber."

"How do you know that?"

"I just do!"

"Well, you're right. But even they complained about it, though for a different reason. They liked to grumble that I wasn't training them how to fight other cavalrymen."

"I don't understand."

"They think that a cavalryman facing a cavalryman is the noblest form of combat. But the purpose of a horseman isn't to engage other horsemen. It's to deliver a shock to enemy infantry. Flank them, break their line and open them up for your own infantry. If a cavalryman finds himself fencing with another cavalryman, he's at the wrong place on the battlefield."

"I saw some troopers exercising once. At an open area just north of Mr. Devlin's ranch. It was so exciting! They were charging in groups of four. Their sabers were raised and pointed forward. They had their wrists turned and the edges of the blades were facing up."

"*In tierce point.*"

"I wish I could do that."

"Go get my saber."

I just stared at him. I knew he had to be joking.

"Do it," he said.

I raced to the house. Mother was rolling out dough for a pie and said something I hardly heard. I grabbed the saber and ran back out.

Mac took the saber and pulled it from its metal sheath.

"Be careful, it's sharp." He handed it to me.

It was heavy. The long curved blade had a single fuller to lighten it, but that did not seem to help much. The brass handguard protected a grip wrapped with calfskin and brass wire.

"Is it too heavy for you?"

"No, I can do it."

"All right, trooper, attention!"

I stood straight as a fence post.

"First I'll teach you The Carry. Left hand relaxed by your side. Now raise the blade vertically and place the back of it

against the hollow of your right shoulder. Drop your right arm more. Keep it about ninety percent extended down your right side. Make sure the left side of the grip and your thumb are against your thigh and your little finger is on the back of the grip. That's it—perfect!"

I was beaming.

"Now The Present Saber. Keep the blade vertical and bring your saber hand around in front of your neck and hold it about six inches in front of it with the edge of the blade to the left. Keep the blade in line with your nose. There, that's the way. Make sure your thumb is extended on the back of the grip and your little finger is alongside your other ones. Excellent!"

I was certain my smile could have lit the entire valley.

"Besides being the way you present the saber, it's also an informal salute between comrades—and sometimes even between adversaries."

"Thank you, Mac."

"Enough for the day?"

I hesitated and he read my mind.

"No," he said. "My lieutenant must learn one more thing."

I held my breath.

"*In tierce point*—mounted."

"Oh, Mac!" I set down the saber. "I'll get Dollar!"

"Whoa! You can't go waving a blade around Dollar's head. He isn't used to that. We'll use Reba."

I ran over to her.

"Wait. Never mount a tethered horse, Katy. If she spooks, you could get killed."

He slipped the quick-release knot from the rail and led her away from the corral. Then he boosted me onto her bare back while he held the lead line. I took a fistful of Reba's mane with my left hand and gripped her with my legs.

"Ready?"

"Yes, sir."

He picked up the saber from the ground and handed it to

me.

"If it gets too heavy, let me know."

"I will."

"All right, raise it, rotate your wrist, and point forward with the blade edge upward. Good. Now throw your right shoulder as far back as you can and bring your elbow to the rear. Lean forward just a little bit at the waist. That's it. All the way. Thrust! Extend that arm! Good. Now back. Thrust again! Perfect! Again!"

The saber seemed twice as heavy after the third thrust. Sweat rolled down my face, and the muscles in the back of my arm were burning. But I felt magnificent. I was no longer a little girl on her mount. I was one with horse and blade. I and the saber and Reba—fused into a single extraordinary being. My arm was screaming in pain, but I would have died rather than lower that blade.

"Well done. She's feared across the Sonoran wastes—and is, withal, the most beautiful trooper in all of Apacheria!"

My eyes must have been flooded with love as I gazed down at him. He extended his right hand and I gave him the saber.

I slid off Reba and he took her to the corral. When he came back, I threw my arms around him. I held him in a death grip until he bent down and I felt his lips press against the top of my head. I eased my arms away and looked up into his eyes.

"Tell me about the cavalry, Mac."

"That's a tall order," he said, laughing.

We sat down together in the shade.

"It's the most romantic arm in the military," he said. "And the most misunderstood."

"Why?"

"I suppose because you have to belong to the cavalry to grasp it fully. Storytellers romanticize us, the infantry resents us, everyone—."

"Resents you? Why?"

"Well, for one, because we get to ride. They ignore the fact that we walk far more than we ride. Horse soldiers don't get to

spend very much time in the saddle—certainly not as much as we'd like. And it rankles the infantry that the dime novelists like to portray us as modern knights. Dashing cavaliers. That always gives the foot sloggers ulcers."

I giggled.

"And they know that if there are pretty girls nearby, they always choose the cavalrymen."

I felt myself blushing.

"But make no mistake, Querida, the cavalry deserves its acclaim."

Of course it does. Mac was one of them. "Tell me why," I said almost in a whisper.

"Because it's the toughest arm of the military. Every task the infantry has to master, we have to master, too. Every dirty job that's theirs is also ours. But besides all that, we have one other enormous charge they don't even have to think about. We have to master the horse. And not a plough horse or a pleasure mount. A warhorse. And not just one, but any and all they throw our way."

I heard the front door open and close, and mother joined us beneath the tree.

"Mac is telling me about the horse soldiers."

She smiled and sat beside me. "Don't let me interrupt," she said to Mac.

His eyes smiled back at her, and then he turned to me.

"If you're around soldiers long enough, Fireball, you'll see that cavalrymen are always more tired than infantrymen. Can you guess why?"

I shook my head no.

"Because our day is never finished. Our horse is always there, always kicking up dust in our mind. We can't rest completely. Ever. Horses are thousand-pound children. They stumble into all sorts of mischief. Get a hundred kinds of injuries and ailments, big and small. If our horse bows a tendon or caps a hock, we're there fretting over him. Tattoo and taps have no

meaning for us. If he colics at three in the morning, we're in the stable trying to get him up and yelling for the veterinarian. Our horse is whinnying and snorting at the back of our mind every day of our lives. Until the day he dies. And then we weep—and the next day we begin all over again."

He turned away and gazed at Reba dozing on her feet in the corral.

"So if a civilian doffs his hat to me when he sees the crossed sabers, I take it as a tribute earned."

Mother sighed and slid an arm around me and pulled me closer to her. We just sat there in silence with the soft breeze caressing us.

Finally Mac turned back to us and smiled, wearily I think, but with a pride few men ever know.

"I think Colonel Hargrave is doing better with his men," I said. "Don't you, Mac?"

Mother kissed me on the side of the head. "My daughter," she said with a smile. "The eternal optimist."

"But don't you, Mac?"

"I do. But I always knew he could."

"You showed him how," I said.

"No, I just held a torch in the darkness for a moment. He had to walk the path himself. Alone."

"It must not be easy," mother said.

"The ability to lead is an odd talent," Mac said. "And so rare that if I could bottle it, I could live on silks and velvet. Yet when you see it in action, it looks so easy. Your first impulse is to discount it as something hardly worth noticing. But when leadership is poor—which is almost always—it visits Hell upon everyone. Even the hapless leader."

"So how do you acquire it?" mother asked.

"You don't. You can't. You can only enhance what's already there."

"Lord, that's not very hopeful."

"Hope isn't my trade, Mary."

"But you can get your men to love you," I said. "That helps."

Mac smiled indulgently. "And how do you know it helps?"

"Because *your* men love you."

"Do they? How do you know that?"

"I heard one say it."

"Did you?" he said in surprise. "Well, that was never my goal. It can't be."

"But why not?" mother asked.

"Because the affection of my troops was never my job. In fact, it could impede it, because once you have that affection, you never want to risk losing it. And that becomes the most insidious of all corruptions."

I looked at mother. She was staring in wonderment at Mac. By now I fully realized that she was so deeply in love with him that I doubted she took a single breath without thinking about him. But her expression now was different. Admiration lit her face.

"Then how do you do it?" she asked.

"I don't know, Mary. I can't quantify it. But I learned very early what not to do. Officers often try one of two ways to deal with their men. Some try to buy their loyalty with privileges and easy duty and even tangible rewards. That never works for more than about ten minutes. It—."

"Why not?" I asked.

"Katy, don't interrupt," mother snapped.

"Because," Mac said to me, "soldiers will always take what you give them but they'll never respect someone who gives them more than they deserve. The briber is held in contempt. As he should be. The troops are made of nobler steel than that."

"And the other thing?" mother said.

"The martinet." Mac looked at me and did not embarrass me by asking if I knew what that meant. "Martinet was a French officer in the army of Louis XIV. He was famous for his strict training methods for recruits. But training is one thing and day

to day leadership is another. It never works over the long pull."

"Do you know any of those martinets?" I asked.

"I have. Usually they have no battle experience. They try to make up for it with a kind of crazed zeal on the parade ground. Once in a while, though, they *have* tasted war. Those are the worst martinets of all. Absolute fanatics. Jack Hargrave's father was one. He was an insufferable man and a poor commander."

"This is so complex," mother said. "It seems hopeless. And yes, I know hope isn't your trade, but how on earth do you know where to start?"

"Don't appease your men with bribes because they'll scorn you, and don't incite their loathing either, because a soldier who wastes day and night hating is spending too much energy on the wrong thing. Love your men if it's within you to do so, and expect no love in return. But if you earn their respect, they'll follow you and live to retire and you'll die a happy man."

"But if they do love you, you'll die a happier man!" I said.

He smiled. "I suppose you will."

"It sounds so hard," mother said.

"You probably think I'm fifty or so, don't you, Mary? I'm actually twenty-seven. What you see is just years of strain."

Mother laughed and lowered her eyes. What she saw was far more than that.

"The funny thing about leadership is that you can read all the books and still know nothing. The reason is that it's ultimately not about content but about style."

I looked at mother. She seemed as puzzled as I was.

"And that has to be almost an intuitive thing," Mac went on. "It's like the style of your handwriting—once you start thinking about it while you're writing, you wreck it. It just has to flow without thought."

"But there must be some principle," mother said. "Some guiding force."

"Now you see where I'm heading. There is. It's one simple and elemental thing, and if an officer masters it, he's destined for Olympus. It isn't how hard he drills his men, or how many

Apacheria

latrines he has them dig, or how many sopapillas he plies them with. Or even how he leads them in battle, because that's very rare. It's one thing only." Mac smiled. "Can you guess what it is?"

"Oh, stop it and tell us!" mother said good-naturedly.

"It's this," he said and raised a forefinger like a schoolmaster. "It's how you give a command."

He paused for effect and we remained silent.

"The whole world pivots on that."

We stared at him for a moment, and then mother said, "Please show us what you mean."

"An officer can give an order to a trooper and he'll resent it, evade it, do all he can to undermine it. A different officer could have given the same order to the same trooper and he'd have jumped to do it, and stood tall with pride when he'd carried it out. Why?"

"You mean it's simply how he gave the command?" mother said.

"Yes—but there's much that underpins the 'how' of that command."

"Can you explain it so a poor merc owner and her daughter can understand?"

Oddly, those words seemed to surprise him. Suddenly he was no longer the colonel. He gazed at both of us with such affection, even longing, that I could never doubt how he felt about us.

I glanced at mother. She seemed startled—and maybe even frightened. That made no sense at all to me.

"Tell us," mother said, bringing him back to the subject.

"It's a matter of style, but something has to underlie the style, too. First, the trooper has to believe that the order makes sense. Not to him—most of what you tell him won't. He thinks all officers are half-mad. But it has to make sense to you—and he has to see it in your eyes. Soldiers always resent busy work given for no real purpose. Most men would rather wrestle with a

tough job that has meaning—at least to you—than an easy one that's obviously pointless."

"I understand," mother said with a smile and gave me a squeeze. "It's true of little girls, too. At least one of them."

"I always make sense, Mary," he said with a smile. "You know that."

"I do." Her tone was very serious.

"The second thing is that you have to convey to him—by your eyes, your posture, your voice—that you've thought about it a heap. That all the difficulties of the task have been ruminated on and digested by you. You've foreseen and appreciated all the sweat necessary and you're confident he can handle anything that might come up. Of course, you won't have foreseen everything, but you have to lead him to believe you've anticipated most of it. He might be the most confident person in the world, but he still needs the confidence he gets from your own belief in him. I can't overemphasize the importance of that."

"I'll bet you did that all the time," I said.

He smiled and winked at me.

"The last thing is that your manner and tone have to assure him that you'll be there to catch him if he falls. Nothing is more vital." He looked away, as if focusing on something far off. "When I was a young lieutenant, my captain ordered me to handle an issue for him with another officer. A captain in another troop. I did, but the other officer treated me badly. I was furious. I told my captain about it and he brushed me off. Told me I was making too much of nothing. The real reason was that the other officer had powerful connections, and my captain didn't want to risk hurting his career. So I—."

"So you didn't take it lying down," mother said with a knowing smile.

"I was insubordinate as Hell. I told him he should defend me even if I was wrong. For my good and the good of the whole troop. After all, I'd been doing his job for him and he left me hanging by my feet. But he would not relent. The fairy gold of a career was too much for him to risk. He destroyed himself in my eyes that day. I never fully trusted him again."

"And his career?" mother asked.

"I never said anything about what happened except to my two closest friends. But they gabbed about it. It ruined him with the troop and with the regiment. Ultimately he left the army. He ended up a broken down drunken lawyer in Ohio. All for a single act of betrayal."

"He violated a sacred trust," mother said.

"Yes. When you give a command, your trooper has to be able to look into your eyes and know that you could be tortured on the rack and still never abandon him."

"It's a noble calling, isn't it, Mac?" I heard myself say, and I suddenly felt as if I were twenty years old.

"It is, Katherine. Oh, and there's one more thing I almost forgot. When you order a man to do something, never tell him how to do it. No soldier wants to be some officer's hand puppet. Let him startle you with his cleverness. You'll end up with a job better done and a proud soldier—and more loyalty than you could buy with a slab of gold."

I grinned at him.

"And when you say your prayers tonight, sweetheart, thank God for the cavalry, because the cavalry forges the finest officers of all." He looked at me with the love my father must have had when he had gazed at me in the cradle. "Do you know why, pretty horsewoman?"

I shook my head no.

"Because of their mastery of the horse. God's own mount. Leading men is like riding a tough horse over rough terrain. Give the horse his head and let him pick his way. If he veers off too much, lay a rein gently against his neck and lead him back on course. Like horses, like men. Be firm of command but light of touch, and give him his head—and he will always take you home."

18

On rainy and wind-whipped nights, mother loved to read me tales and poems of Edgar Allan Poe. Mother was a cultured woman by any standards one cared to use, though she concealed it as being no one else's business. In a place where the most hotly debated topic might be the best rifle caliber for varmint hunting, mother had rows of books she used as doorways for me to other worlds.

I thought of Mr. Poe on this balmy Sunday afternoon, because mother was taking a nap. This was a startling circumstance. She almost never napped. Like her favorite author, she considered sleep to be "little slices of death." And, like Poe, she would sometimes say, "How I loathe them."

Yet now she was out. Exhausted, I think, not by tasks performed, but by emotions felt. I stood in the doorway of her room and looked at her. Mother was a pretty sleeper. Lord knows, many were not. She was lovely there, full clothed and adorning the bed in the half-light. I sighed as I watched her. I was at the age when a girl begins to feel her mother is cramping her a bit, taking too much slack out of the reins. We had already had a few tests of will, and I had tried to buck her off, without success. "You're just like me," she had said without anger after one such dust-up. I knew she was right, though I had not been willing to admit it. In truth, I did not want to spat with mother or battle mother — I wanted to *be* mother.

Apacheria

I closed her door quietly and wandered outside. Mac had ridden to town to talk over some things with Sheriff Blaine. The afternoon was all mine. I moseyed around doing nothing until I heard hoofbeats and saw Timmy riding up. I smiled and ran over to him with an eagerness that would have embarrassed me a few weeks earlier.

"Let's have a picnic," he said. "I have some carne seca and tortillas."

Timmy was never big on preliminaries. That had always seemed odd to me. About a decade later I woke up in the middle of the night and it suddenly hit me why. The abrupt brutality of his life had outlawed elaborate niceties. Deep down he had always feared there was simply no time.

"That sounds like fun," I said.

"Get your horse."

"Why?"

"Let's go down to the river."

I hesitated. "Do you think that's all right?"

"Sure. Besides, I have my .22."

If Mac had been right, then the Apaches were nowhere near and we had nothing to fear.

"I'm not so sure. . . ."

"Come on. It's a perfect day."

Timmy seemed to be growing taller by the hour. He had bought some new clothes and had even gotten a haircut. And he looked irresistibly masculine up there in the saddle.

"Come on, Katy. It'll be fun."

"All right," I said with a grin.

He dismounted and handed me the reins. "I'll tack up Dollar for you."

As on every day in summer, the San Pedro was gorgeous. We tied up our horses on a picket line between two cottonwoods—Timmy was always very serious about how he tethered his mounts—and we spread a blanket and got out the chow. We startled some toads and salamanders that went

splashing or scurrying off, and we sat on the blanket and just enjoyed the food and the peacefulness.

Timmy had laid his small rifle on the blanket between us. I was about to slide it out of the way when he pressed a hand down onto it and stopped me. I knew then that he meant it as a symbol.

"Katy, I have to ask you something."

"Sure."

He was staring straight ahead, as though he were afraid to look at me. "May I wait for you?"

"Wait? What do you mean?"

He was still looking forward instead of at me. "Until you're older. Until you're of age."

I had no idea how to answer that.

"I know I'm too old for you now. But that'll change in a few years. I'll wait those years. As many years as you want. And I'll never look at another girl."

"Oh, Timmy...."

"And I'll never touch you." He turned to me. "I give you my pledge of honor."

His words were lost on me, because his gaze had suddenly made me feel flushed. I was shaking all over as I moved my right hand across the blanket and slid it into his. It was so warm, so powerful and good. I felt it all the way down to my toes.

I started to speak, but my words tripped over themselves in my mouth. I stopped and cleared my throat. Then in a gentle whisper, I said, "Please wait for me."

His light brown eyes showed a special joy I had never seen in eyes before. Then he did something that overwhelmed me. He kissed the tips of the first two fingers of his right hand and reached across the rifle and touched them gently to my forehead. I knew at that moment I would be with him for the rest of my life.

A cactus wren screeched to my left. Two or three others joined in until I just wanted to swat them for annoying me now.

"Don't move," Timmy said.

Apacheria

"Why not?"

"Still!" he commanded.

I froze.

"They're not doing that for no reason. There's probably a snake in the brush next to you."

I turned my head slowly. Sure enough, a big diamondback glided silently out from beneath the scrub and coiled up on a nice sunny patch to bask. The problem was that it was only about a foot from my left hand. The snake seemed unaware of us, or simply indifferent.

I knew enough about snakes to realize that if it did not feel threatened, it would not strike. The best thing for me to do would be to wait until it moved off. But it seemed settled into its warm spot now with no intention of obliging.

"Slide toward me slowly," Timmy said. "No fast movements."

I shifted my weight, but that was enough. The snake exploded into action, its head launching into a high arched coil and its rattle shouting at me to beware.

"Stop!" Timmy said. He slid off the blanket with his rifle in his left had. "Don't move." He made a wide circle and came up around the snake from another direction. "I'll distract it and you get away."

He began waving the rifle around in front of the animal's face, but the snake's harsh little eyes still focused on me.

"No!" I shouted as Timmy got even closer so the snake would turn toward him. "He'll get you!"

"Move out!"

I knew at that moment that he was willing to sacrifice himself for me. And I also knew that I would do the same for him.

I stood up, daring the snake to strike at me before Timmy could risk himself any further. But my foot slipped on a rock under the blanket and I tripped and yelped as I twisted my ankle hard as I hit the ground. I looked up. The snake's head was no

more than a foot from my face. The rattling seemed deafening.

"I can't stand up!" I shouted to Timmy.

"Don't move."

I tore my eyes from the snake and looked at Timmy. His small rifle was up at his shoulder, but the barrel was shaking like a twig in the wind. There was no hope he could hit anything at all.

And then the rattler's head was gone. Vanished to vapor before me. It seemed like minutes passed before I realized my ears were ringing with gunfire.

Timmy stared in disbelief and so did I. There was no smoke rising from his weapon. But the headless snake lay before me.

The softest footsteps approached through the brush. I looked up. A giant of a figure towered over me and led a magnificent paint horse by the reins. The bright sky beyond made the man a black silhouette as tall as an oak. He gestured to Timmy, and Timmy lowered his rifle. Then he turned and dropped to one knee before me and laid his carbine upon the ground. In the dappled light, I could see him at last.

A russet face as dark as a well-aged gun scabbard confronted me. Deep eyes looked into my soul. His cheekbones were so prominent that sparrows could have fluttered beneath them and sheltered in the shadows. A long, sharp nose fit perfectly with all the rest.

Shoulder length black hair streaked with strands of silver framed the man's face. A red silk bandana encircled his forehead and kept all that hair neat. In the wilds of southern Arizona he was as clean and crisp as if he had just prepared himself for a studio portrait.

But it was to his eyes that I had to return. They were gray or hazel, I was not quite sure, and their casual power entranced me. He examined me with a relaxed intensity. Oddly, his eyes not only gazed at me but simultaneously seemed to look back inward, as if he were observing the world and reflecting upon it at the same time.

Apacheria

I began to stand, and the pain in my ankle flooded me with nausea. Suddenly the color bled out of my surroundings. Everything went gray.

"I'm going to be sick," I said and threw up all over myself. I fell to my knees and kept retching.

He let me finish and then picked me up as if I were a doll and set me on the ground away from the soiled blanket. He tore up some grasses and made a soft bed for me and placed me on it.

"*Hombre*," he said to Timmy in a voice that rolled like thunder, and he pulled the red bandana from his head.

Timmy ran over and he handed him the silk.

"*Agua*."

Timmy hurried down to the riverbank.

The man wore a buckskin shirt and trousers and black cavalry boots. A stag-handled hunting knife hung from his right hip. When Timmy returned, the man took the bandana and sliced it in half. Then he made a gesture for Timmy to turn around.

The rancid slop all over my shirt front was disgusting. He began unbuttoning my shirt. At my age, as I was just beginning to bud, I should have been embarrassed, even ashamed. But I felt nothing like that at all. He slid the shirt from my shoulders and threw it aside. Then he took one of the wet bandana halves and wiped me gently. When he had finished, he tossed it away and took the other one and filled it with some yellow blossoms. He rubbed the silk vigorously between his hands until it was saturated with perfume. Then he wiped me down again until I smelled as sweet as this summer day.

By the time he was done, I was shivering with a chill. He pulled off his shirt and slipped the buckskin over me. Soon I felt as comfortable as if I were in my own bed.

He laid me back onto the grass and pulled off my boot and sock and examined my ankle. I flinched when he touched it.

He took his knife and cut my trouser leg up as far as the knee. With delicate fingers, he explored the muscles and nerves

just below my knee and pressed gently. The pain in my ankle began to ease. It did not go away completely, but it became just an annoyance rather than the agony it had been only minutes earlier.

He looked down at me and smiled with those mysterious eyes.

I felt my lower lip start to quiver, and I knew I was about to cry. I pushed myself up. I tried to encircle him with my arms and I pressed my face against a chest that felt like iron.

"Manolete," I whispered and struggled to hold back my tears. He held me up as I hugged him as hard as I could.

I was in the arms of the most feared man in all the Southwest, and I felt nothing but gratitude and wonder.

I sat back and just stared at him.

"You look deeply."

I jumped with a start, because he spoke flawless English, with a lush mixture of accents that I had not heard before. And then it occurred to me that never in my entire life had I spoken with a full-blooded Apache.

"Thank you for helping us," I said.

He continued to gaze into my soul. With another, it might have been a violation, even obscene. But not with this man.

I looked away and then saw something that made my heart leap.

"I know him," I said, smiling and pointing to the Winchester.

He looked down at the carbine. "Him?"

"The man who gave it to you." I pointed to the "RM" carved into a corner of the stock. "Those are his initials."

Manolete picked up the rifle and ran a finger over the letters incised on the walnut. Suddenly I felt stupid. His look of puzzlement told me he had no idea what I meant. How could he? The Apaches possessed no written language. "Initials" meant nothing to him.

"Those are symbols that stand for his name," I said. "Redmond McGregor."

Apacheria

It was as if I had uttered a strange incantation. His eyes swept over me and glittered with the ripple and flow of the entire history of his life. All from the simple mention of a man's name.

"He is your father?" he asked, gazing at my red hair and freckles.

"Oh, I wish he—." I caught myself and felt very guilty. "He's my friend. My father is dead."

"Indeh?"

"No."

He seemed relieved.

"He's staying with us. With me and my mother."

Who would have guessed that an Apache could smile? I thought it was against the law.

"*El Pelo Canoso.*"

"Yes," I said, laughing. "Silver Hair. But it's white now."

"You respect him." It was not a question.

"Yes."

"And love him."

"Yes.

"He told you about Manolete?"

"Yes. And how he still carries your arrowhead."

"Carries?"

"In his shoulder. *Incrustado.*"

A hint of fierceness sharpened his smile. "That was long ago."

"I know."

"Does he still hate?"

I could never have lied to this man. "He says he does."

"Good. Hate is pure. And sometimes all we have."

"But I don't believe him."

Now Manolete's smile was gentle and soft and only for me. He reached across and brushed some hairs away from my eyes. "You are too young to know the glory of hate, Coloradita. May you never know it."

I touched his brown hand on my forehead and wrapped my fingers around his.

"*Hombre,*" he said, turning to the boy I was beginning to love.

Timmy stood up. He seemed pleased that Manolete had called him *hombre* instead of *niño*.

"Get this girl's mother and bring her here in a wagon. Tell her to bring no soldiers. No McGregor."

Timmy hesitated.

"Please," I said to Timmy. "I'm safe here."

Timmy mounted his horse and rode off.

I touched Manolete's right arm, and he looked back at me.

"Colonel McGregor is retired. He isn't a soldier anymore."

That confused him. "Retired?"

"Yes. *Jubilado.*"

"*No entiendo.* That is like saying Manolete is no longer Indeh. How can this be?"

I did not know how to answer.

He stared off down the river. "Then all are less safe in this land. Perhaps even Indeh."

He said not another word. We sat together in silence until we heard the creak of a buckboard.

Manolete grabbed his carbine and stood up. He raised the weapon to his right shoulder, but his left arm hung relaxed at his side. I had never seen anyone hold a rifle one-handed like that.

Timmy came running through the cottonwoods, and mother was right behind him.

Manolete lowered the rifle.

I limped toward her and she rushed forward. Her arms encircled me like a suit of chain mail.

In a burst, I told her everything that had happened, though Timmy certainly already had.

She eased her arms off me and stepped slowly up to Manolete.

I was sure I saw a smile in his eyes. And I was certain of the reason, too. He knew he was looking at the bravest woman alive.

Apacheria

She reached out and took his left hand. She lowered her head—something I head never seen her do to any man—and raised his hand to her lips and pressed them to the backs of his fingers.

"Thank you," she whispered.

He nodded and she released him.

They stared at one another for a moment, and then mother said, "Where will you go now?"

"We remain here until the dark moon. Then we move off."

He glanced at me and then turned and walked toward his horse.

"God bless you," mother said.

He stopped and looked back. "*Estás una Cristiana?*"

"*Sí.*"

"Thank your Christ for this little one."

"I do. Every day."

"She looks deeply. Wisely. And justly. Your Christ has breathed the spirit of Indeh across her soul. Only *un Gran Espíritu* can do that."

Then he sprang into the saddle of his paint and was gone.

19

I was bursting to tell Mac everything. Mother and I rode back in the buckboard, and Timmy rode his own horse and ponied Dollar behind him.

As we rolled up to the house, I saw that Reba was not in the corral.

"Look," Timmy said.

A dust cloud approached from the west. Soon we could hear the hoofbeats. Skeels and Lomaddis came into view at the head of about a dozen riders. Bandits all. They were Indian hunting. Or so they claimed.

I waited for mother to help me down, but she stayed on the seat, so I did not move.

"Howdy, neighbor," Lomaddis said as they pulled up.

"Why are you here?" mother asked.

"Some greeeeeting," Lomaddis answered in his eerie, drawn out way.

Looking for sign," Skeels said. "We've heard rumors about Apaches on the move."

"Get off my land," mother said.

"Not nice, Mary," Clete answered. "We're here to protect white people."

"You're out to commit crimes and blame it on Indians!" I shouted.

"Katy!" mother snapped.

That startled Lomaddis, and he turned to Skeels. The scalphunter glared at me with the look of a hungry cur.

Mother reached under the seat and pulled out her shotgun. She laid it across her lap and cocked both barrels. The two metallic clicks were as unmistakable as a pair of funeral prayers.

"You're trespassers. Get off my land now." Her eyes bored into Skeels. "If I smell you here again, I'll blow you out of the saddle."

I knew she meant it. Mother never bluffed. To protect her cub, she would have taken him down without a thought.

I looked back at Timmy. His rifle was tight to his shoulder and pointing at Skeels' face.

"Let's ride!" Skeels said and bolted off.

His killers ate the dust behind him.

Mother gently lowered the hammers on the shotgun. "Timmy, you'll stay for supper."

"Thank you, Mrs. Malone, but I have to work this afternoon."

He slid his rifle into its scabbard and dismounted. He came over to the wagon and extended his arms upward to me. I began to climb down, and he gripped me above the waist. Even through the buckskin I could feel his strong fingers against my ribs. He set me softly down.

"I can never be your hero like the colonel is, but I'll always be here for you." He gazed at me as if I were an object of worship.

"You're all the hero I'll ever need," I whispered. Then even lower so mother could not hear, I said. "I'll be your wife someday. Please wait for me."

The joy in his eyes overwhelmed me, but he was also shaking so much I worried that mother might notice and wonder why. He hurried to his horse and was gone before I could say another word.

Dumbstruck is not a feature of the Irish race. Yet Mac sat there immobile and speechless as I finished my tale.

"What power you have over men, Katherine," he said finally.

I was not sure if he meant Manolete or him or the boy I now loved.

"How did he look?" Mac asked mother.

"Very fit. But weary, I think. Melancholy."

Mac sighed. "There is no one sadder than a sad Apache."

"We didn't see any braves," I said. "He was all alone."

"I'm sure that's true, Fireball. You didn't see any. But they were there."

"What shall we do?" mother asked.

"About what?"

"About him."

"How do you mean?"

"Everyone is hunting him down. The army. The scalphunter and his barbarians. Anyone with a rifle."

"What do you want to do?"

"To help him live," mother and I said at the same time.

Mac looked at her without sentiment. "Are you sure that's what you want for this savage? Certain?"

"Yes!" she said with a hint of anger.

Mac smiled. "Good. Because I am certain, too."

Both of us just stared at him.

"Saddle up!"

"Now?" mother said.

"Now."

"But how will we find him?" I asked.

Mac laughed. "We won't have to."

Southern Arizona often shocks people. Visiting the same place at different times of the day is like entering unconnected

worlds. The soft balminess of the San Pedro in the morning gives no hint of the area in late afternoon. Then the low sun angles its rays like sharp blades through the cottonwoods. The pleasing colors of morning give way to deep contrasts of light and dark that can seem unwelcoming, even ominous.

We rode along the bank in the half light and came upon the blanket and my discarded shirt on the ground where I had left them. Mac raised his right hand. I pulled up next to his left, and mother stopped on his right.

He peered upstream along this river of shadows. I could make out nothing unusual. I looked at Mac. His expression was one I had never seen before. I was not sure it was one of pleasure—to this day I am still not sure. Yet I think I saw satisfaction there, but of a sort I could scarcely understand. Perhaps it was of a kind savored only by warriors old and scarred.

I gazed back up the river. What at first had seemed a shadow now I saw was a man. Mac nudged Reba gently forward and we followed.

Manolete stood with his arms folded across his bare chest. No carbine could be seen, but his hunting knife hung at his hip. We stopped about ten feet away.

"I knew you would come," Manolete said, lowering his arms.

"How did you know?"

"All that has happened is the result of a power greater than you or I." His eyes turned to me, and a tiny smile curled his dark lips. "Even greater than the brave Coloradita."

Suddenly his head snapped to his left and his right hand leaped to his knife. Mother had reached back to her saddlebag.

"Stop!" Mac said to her.

"I brought you something," she said to Manolete.

His hand eased off his knife.

Mother pulled out a maroon fireman's shirt and extended it toward him. "Against the chill."

He came forward and took it.

I felt Dollar tense and saw his ears move. Off to the right, two Apache braves on foot emerged from the shadows. Both held repeating rifles.

Manolete turned and walked off into the shadows. We dismounted and led our horses behind him. Darkness had enveloped us by the time we entered a small clearing. I was surprised Manolete was incautious enough to have a campfire, when all mankind seemed to be hunting him, but there it was. Some of the tallest cottonwoods in Arizona surrounded us. We had indeed stepped into a separate world.

We let our horses graze and went to the fire. Manolete offered us no food because there was none, but mother remedied that. From her saddlebag she produced a slab of smoked ham and handed it to him. The expressions on the faces of the two braves screamed of their hunger. Manolete hesitated and looked at Mac.

"She is a woman of honor," Mac said.

Manolete's caution was understandable. After all, Indians had been poisoned before.

He handed the meat to his men and said a few words in his own tongue. They began cutting up the meat and eating it immediately. Manolete seemed immune to hunger.

We sat around the fire, and the two old adversaries eyed each other over the flames.

"You have come why?" Manolete said at last.

"I think you know."

"To honor me in this grand refuge?" he said with a contemptuous sweep of his hand.

"To help you survive."

"You are too late, Canoso. All Indeh are long dead. Husks have no life."

"The whole world wants you dead."

"I *am* dead."

"Have I wasted my time then?"

"You have wasted your life."

Apacheria

It was a terrible thing for Manolete to say. I looked at mother and then at Mac. There was no anger in Mac's eyes. Only sadness.

"Wait!" mother said when Mac began to stand up. "We want to help you."

"Why?"

She hesitated and then said, "Because I'm a woman of honor."

Manolete smiled for the first time this night and looked at Mac. "You have chosen wisely. Sit."

Mac dropped back down Indian style.

"Why did you leave the agency?" Mac asked.

"You have heard the story."

"Why did you leave?"

"To stop myself from killing and bringing ruin on my people. But that was a mistake."

"It was a mistake not to let your people be killed?" mother asked, clearly shocked. She was the only woman I knew who would interrupt two men in conversation—and such men as these!

"Yes," Manolete answered.

"That's horrible," mother said.

He gazed at her as if she were a small child. "If I could, I would kill all Indeh. Today."

"Explain what you mean," Mac said, though it was obviously for our benefit, not his own.

Manolete's patient eyes were more understanding than any Apache's were supposed to be.

"When a dog is too sick to live, you kill it, do you not? When its legs no longer work or it vomits the blood from its body. You kill it to end misery. Killing becomes mercy."

Mother seemed too bewildered to speak, but at last she said, "Is there no hope then?"

He looked at Mac with a tired smile. "She *is* a woman of honor." He turned back to her. "Indeh are warriors since the

beginning of time. Now the fathers in Washington have put us in a big corral and told us to scrape the earth and drop horse dung on the scrapings. We are to scatter seeds and wait. Indeh warriors are to sit on the ground and watch shoots grow out of horse dung. The Washington fathers are fools and the sons of fools."

Mother turned away, unable to answer the unanswerable.

"Listen. . . ." he said, and mother looked back at him.

"For Indeh, the greatest of all joys is to exert their will. It is life and the breath of life. The will to tame a wild horse. Or a wild woman. To create noble sons and honorable daughters. To seize the horses of our enemies and the friends of our enemies. To lay waste their fields. To destroy *their* will."

"But how —."

"And Indeh will was the most powerful force on earth — until it clashed with the will of the longknives."

Mother remained quiet.

"For Indeh, will is all." He looked at Mac. "And now the bluecoats have outlawed all."

Silence followed except for a coyote and his sad song far up the river.

"But Colonel McGregor is your friend," mother said. "And so are Katy and I."

Manolete smiled. "A formidable army, I am sure, but with more will than wisdom."

"Please let us help you," she said.

"What is there to help?" he asked. "We have reached the end of our line. We are—" he turned to Mac—"*Cómo se dice los caballos castrados?*"

"Geldings," Mac said.

"Indeh have become geldings. The end is at hand."

"No!" mother said. "I won't accept that."

"Or perhaps we can return to the agency and will plants to grow from *la mierda*. That would be will indeed."

"Stop it!" mother said.

Apacheria

Manolete smiled at Mac. "I see where Coloradita gets her fire."

"How many left the agency with you?" Mac asked.

"Seven. When we rode to Mexico, two stayed in Arizona to raid at their pleasure."

"If there are any more killings, Sheridan will be furious," Mac said.

"Yes."

"Crook won't be able to hold him back."

"The Gray Fox is here?"

"Nearby."

"A great war chief. He has never lied to us. And he has always fought with honor."

"And much will."

"Yes. Much will."

"Where are your other three men?"

"*Rurales.*"

Mac nodded. "What are your plans?"

"What are yours?"

"To watch you die a miserable death, or to see you get back to San Carlos where your people need you. Your choice."

"Bravely spoken."

"Your call."

"Why help Manolete?"

"So I can go to my grave without having to say I wasted my life."

That hit Manolete hard. I could see it in his eyes. It had been a fierce cut he had delivered to his old enemy, and he knew now it had been a cut without honor.

Manolete rose and his two men behind him did also. He came around to our side of the fire. Mac stood up and Manolete gripped both his upper arms.

"*Ch' oondé.*"

"Yes," Mac said.

"Let me think this night. We will speak again tomorrow."

193

Not a word passed among us on the way home. When we reached the house, I tended the horses and mother went to get a fire going for some hot tea.

Mac was in the big chair when I got inside. He had opened the bottle of tequila Colonel Hargrave had given him. The almost empty glass told me that he was ready for the second round.

Mother and I sat across from him on the sofa and sipped our tea. Somehow it tasted bitter to me, and I set it aside.

Mac seemed suddenly old. Beyond old, even. Ancient. One of those marble Roman portrait busts of some once-hallowed general that Miss Hentz had told us about in school. Chipped and cracked and darkened with the patina of antiquity.

And looking at that hint of ruin cursed me with a monstrous guilt.

Children are the most selfish people on earth. They have to be. Otherwise they could not survive to adulthood. Now I knew I was reaching childhood's end. At that moment, I wished Mac had never met us. Never looked at me, never saw me smile. I wished he had kept riding. No Manolete, no haunted memories, no reminders of his key role in the conquest of a mighty race. I loved him as profoundly as a girl can love a man who is not her father, and now because of that I wished I had never known him. I loved him that much. This night of great pain for him was also the moment I began to tip-toe fearfully toward womanhood.

"It's not your fault, Redmond," mother said gently. "I see it in your eyes, but you're wrong."

"How can a man like that be reduced to such a state?" He poured himself more tequila. "Once he was lord of the desert. Now he hides among the lizards and toads. God have mercy. Mercy on me."

"It's the sweep of history," mother said. "We're all caught up in it."

Apacheria

"No," Mac said. "I *made* the history. And someday I'll have to answer for it."

"Oh, stop it!" I said, jumping up and forgetting I was almost a woman. I ran to him and leaped into his lap. The glass of tequila went flying as I threw my arms around him and kissed him on the cheek and just held. I had never kissed him before.

"Oh, Katy," he whispered. I could hear the tears in his voice. He pulled my head to his chest and held me there.

"Stop hurting yourself," I pleaded with him.

His lips pressed against my hair. "I can't believe there was a time when you weren't part of my life. Both of you."

I sneaked a look at mother. She was smiling, but it was a melancholy smile. That baffled me.

Mac slid me off his lap and stood up. He walked toward his room without saying goodnight. He had never done that before.

"Mac?"

I half expected him not to hear me, but he stopped and turned. It was the old general's face, the battered Roman marble.

"What does *ch' oondé* mean?"

He hesitated, then said, "It means friend."

Then he turned and walked away with the weariness and finality of a man on the edge of Judgment Day.

20

I was certain I would not sleep that night. Yet I barely remember my head touching the pillow.

I woke at first light. The songs of birds and the sound of mother's deep breathing beside me filled my ears. The smell of fresh coffee told me Mac was already up.

I washed and dressed without waking mother and closed the door quietly behind me.

Mac was sitting at the dining table with his coffee. He was a different man than when I had last seen him. He seemed refreshed and alert. Revived by drawing on what resources I could not imagine. Those almost feminine aqua eyes, so disconcertingly beautiful in that sun scored face, glittered with new energy. Woe to the ungodly on this fateful day.

He was wearing his dark blue fireman's shirt and black trousers. His nickel-plated Colt nestled in the shoulder holster under his left arm.

He smiled at me and I melted, as I had every day since I had first met him.

"Sit with me, Katy," he said, but I did not need to be asked. "When your mother wakes up, tell her I've gone to Huachuca. I'm going to ask Jack Hargrave to leash the dogs of war for now. Give Manolete some running room so—."

"But you don't even know yet what Manolete is going to decide to do."

Mac was always tolerant when I interrupted him. "It doesn't matter. He doesn't have the luxury to dawdle over this. And I don't have the luxury to wait. I have to move now."

He stood up and reached for his old army hat. "What's the matter?"

I lowered my eyes.

"What is it?" he said.

I looked up at him. "Thank you."

"For what?"

"For everything." My lips were dry, and all of a sudden I felt very scared.

He came around to my side of the table and leaned against the edge and gazed down at me. "Tell me."

"You're just like my father."

He looked puzzled. "I thought you never knew him."

"No, no, I mean you're just *like a father*. To me. You love me and hug me and . . . . I mean . . . ."

He slid his left hand around my neck and rubbed his thumb up and down the back of my head. "What's wrong? You act like you're never going to see me again."

"It's just that . . . people are so evil."

"Don't say that. *Some* people are evil. But not many. Most are just people—halfway between good and bad."

"But no one wants to help you."

"No one?"

"Just a few."

"That's an army. Jack Hargrave is worth any ten men. And Jim Blaine at least eight."

"I'm scared for you. And for Manolete."

He smoothed down my hair. "It wouldn't do for my little girl to give in to her fears. I'll bet you never have before."

"Am I really? Am I your little girl?" I reached up and grabbed his wrist and squeezed it. "Am I like . . . ?"

"A daughter?"

"Yes," I whispered.

"Katy, you're the daughter from Heaven."

I could no longer speak.

He leaned down and kissed me on top of the head. "I'll be back as fast as Reba can carry me."

He put on his hat and left without another word.

Reba's hoofbeats must have woken mother. She came out of her room sleepy-faced and still buttoning her dressing gown.

I told her where Mac had gone. She gave me a good morning kiss and hugged me a little longer than usual. She said nothing as she made me some tea and helped herself to the coffee.

We sat in silence for a spell.

"We're not going to open the merc today," she said at last. "Make some flapjack batter while I get dressed."

"I'm not very hungry, mom."

"It's for the Apaches," she said, going back to her room. "Those men are hungry out there."

We made our way to the San Pedro with our picnic basket loaded with flapjacks and ham. Mother was being very cautious. Besides placing the shotgun under the buckboard seat, she had buckled on her Schofield.

The bright sun soon began to burn off the chill and the early morning dampness. I knew the noisy buckboard would alert Manolete long before we reached the edge of the cottonwoods, so I was surprised he was not there to meet us. Mother pulled up and waited.

The birds were especially loud this morning, and the wrens sounded insane—the way they were when they spotted a snake.

"Wellllll," a familiar voice said, and I learned that day that the wrens knew their business.

Lomaddis had come out of a bend in the trees to our right.

"No, no," he said when mother's hand dropped to her hip. "No firearms. I've never killed a woman, but I'll do what's necessary. And that includes the little viper tongue next to you."

Two middle-aged men stepped out from the trees. I recognized them as a couple of hardcases who were friends of Lomaddis. If a man like that could ever be said to have friends.

One of them took our weapons while Lomaddis folded his arms and watched.

"You're lucky we got here before those savages found you," he said to mother.

"Where are they?" she asked.

"Now, what to do . . . ?" he said, stroking his chin. Then he laughed, as though amused by his own theatrics. "Get down!" he shouted.

We climbed out of the buckboard.

"Take it back to their place and put the horse away," he told one of the men. "I want it to look like they never came here."

The man tied his horse to the back of the buckboard and drove off.

"Mary, get on behind Zeke," Lomaddis said. "I'll take the little red-headed rattler with me. If either of you tries to get clever, we'll push you off and stomp you to death right there."

The glare in mother's eyes was terrifying. "Hurt my daughter and I'll hunt you through the streets of Hell."

Lomaddis turned away. "I'll do what's necessary. Let's ride!"

Soon it became clear we were headed for the Dragoon Mountains. The pointed peaks above Cochise Stronghold loomed before us. The Chiricahua Apaches were long gone from there now, except for the great dead chief, resting in eternal solitude.

We passed the rounded mound of Treaty Peak and rode into the stronghold itself. From a distance, the Dragoons appeared jagged. Yet up close, you became overwhelmed by the enormous rounded granite boulders that seemed about to tumble over on

top of you. Only mules could have conquered these fastnesses, were it not for the well worn Apache trails going back in time only God knew how long.

I knew that somewhere nearby was the circle of boulders called Council Rocks, where General Howard had made peace with Cochise. Now we were profaning it with white barbarians.

Finally we came out onto a gorgeous green valley in the heart of the stronghold. About a mile beyond, the valley ended in another narrow pass through the mountains. Off to the right, the floor of the valley rose in a gentle slope with a game trail cutting through the lush grass all the way to the top of the ridge and perhaps beyond.

The sun was low when we reached the center of the valley floor. Skeels had a fire going. I was startled to see Manolete there. He was sitting by the fire with his hands bound behind him. He did not acknowledge us as we approached.

I was sore from riding and happy to dismount. Mother and I were barely off our horses when Zeke tied our hands behind us and pushed us down near the fire.

Manolete remained impassive. He was wearing the maroon fireman's shirt mother had given him, along with his buckskin trousers and cavalry boots. His hunting knife and Winchester lay on the ground near where Zeke was now unrolling a bedroll.

From scraps of conversation, I learned that Skeels and the others had swooped on the Apaches, but Manolete's two braves had escaped while he had made a stand. It sounded as if he had sacrificed himself for both of them. No doubt they were safely on their way back to San Carlos.

"What's the purpose of all this?" mother demanded of Skeels.

He seemed amazed by her question. "Don't you know?"

"How could I?"

"Remember what that little red pepper shouted at us? You know too much. Your time is over."

"You must be mad! Jim Blaine will hunt you down like dogs."

Apacheria

Skeels smiled. "Why? Because we found the corpse of a beautiful woman violated and murdered by this renegade? With her daughter cut down in the crossfire? And the Indian himself shot to death in the final struggle?"

"Whoa!" Lomaddis said. "What are you talking about?"

"What do you think I'm talking about?"

"I don't care what you do with this goddam Apache," Lomaddis said. "But I don't kill women and children."

"Did you think I brought them here just to scare them? If the rest of the men don't get here by tomorrow morning, we'll do the deed then and haul in the corpses. And that'll be it."

"They'll never catch those Apache bucks," Zeke said.

Skeels shrugged. "Maybe not."

"I don't care what you say," Lomaddis said. "I'm not going touch a woman or a little girl."

"Doesn't matter," Skeels said. "I'll crush them like maggots. All white women are maggots. And when I'm done, I'll scrape them off my boots."

"Clete, you can't be part of this," mother said.

He looked horrified, but he was obviously very afraid of Skeels. He unsaddled his horse and took his bedroll and spread it out at the far side of the fire. Then he lay on his side with his back to us and said no more.

Mother looked at Manolete.

He glanced at her as if she were a stranger and then stared off into the gathering night.

"Go to sleep," Skeels said to us.

"At least give us a blanket," mother said.

"What for?"

"Give them a goddam blanket!" Lomaddis shouted without turning around.

Skeels laughed and threw us one that smelled of horse.

"Lie down," he said and pulled it over us.

We stretched out on the thick grass, and I lay like a spoon against mother's back.

201

William Altimari

"Don't worry," I whispered. "Mac is coming. Don't worry."

"Yes," she said, but there was no hope in her voice.

I drifted off from exhaustion. I woke up once in the middle of the night to the sound of mother crying in the darkness. I knew she was crying not for herself, but for me.

I looked around and was surprised to see Manolete still sitting upright in the dying firelight, still staring ahead, communing—I was certain—with his God.

"God damn it!"

I jumped up so fast I got light-headed.

The sun was just starting to peek over the mountains.

Skeels was standing over Zeke. "You stupid, toothless fool!"

Lomaddis joined him near Zeke.

Mother was up now, too, and we pushed ourselves to our knees and then to our feet and went over to them.

Zeke was sleeping peacefully on his back despite the tirade. His throat had been cut by an expert, and he had died without so much as a gurgle.

The Winchester and Apache hunting knife were gone. And so was Manolete. His paint was gone, too. He had walked the horse off in silence. Truly he *was* lord of these lands.

"The Apaches are demons," Lomaddis said, barely above a whisper.

But what was most hideous to me was that Manolete had abandoned us. He had not even tried to help us. He had left his friends to die alone like maggots under a heel.

I looked up at mother. She read my mind.

"I don't know, Scamp." She shook her head over and over. "I don't know."

"End this now," Lomaddis said to Skeels. "Let these two go and let's head to Sonora." He came over and pulled a knife and cut our bonds.

"They can hang us," Skeels said. "Saddle up."

Apacheria

When they were done, Skeels turned toward mother. His godless eyes looked like a pair of tombstones.

"I'll do whatever you want," mother said. "Spare my daughter and I'll never say a word. Please don't hurt my little girl."

Skeels slashed mother with a backhand that sent her sprawling. I kicked him as hard as I could in a knee and he slapped me and I fell backward.

"Gringo trash!" he spat at us. "I hate all of you." He pulled his skinning knife from its sheath. "You'll die slow," he said to mother. "Red scalps bring no money, but they bring me more than that."

"Oh, God," Lomaddis said.

Skeels sneered at him. "No stomach for a man's work?"

But Lomaddis was not looking at us. He was staring at the top of the ridge off to the right. The bright sky behind blackened the lone horseman into a silhouette, but I knew instantly who it was.

"Mac!" I shouted.

Lomaddis bolted toward his gear and his sixshooter, and Skeels dived for mother's Schofield near his bedroll.

"Look!" Mother pointed.

A second horseman rode over the ridge. He hefted a carbine to his right shoulder, but with only one hand. What an odd way to hold a longarm. Yet he held it with the graceful confidence of a man who could shoot the head off a snake inches from a terrified little girl.

And then the horses exploded down the hill.

Gunfire rocked the Dragoons. Lomaddis's horse dropped dead as a stone with a bullet through the head, and the scalphunter's mount bolted across the valley. Nothing else was being hit. All four men were firing and bullets whizzed everywhere to no effect.

Reba flew down the hill like a spirit, but Manolete's paint was even swifter. He closed on the two men.

Skeels and Lomaddis fell back to reload.

I looked at Mac. He must have been empty, because he reholstered his sixgun. He was moving too fast to reload. Yet on he came.

Manolete sheathed his carbine but still he bore down on Lomaddis.

The killers blazed away, and yet the two mad horsemen seemed mindless of death.

The Apache closed, and Lomaddis broke. He raced toward mother and hooked her by the neck and pulled her in front of him like a shield. I jumped on him, but Skeels grabbed me by the hair and wrenched me off his back.

I pulled myself free from his sweaty grip and tried to reach mother.

Manolete pounded by me, so close I could smell the sweat of his horse.

He pulled up and leaped from his paint in a sweeping movement that is indescribable. He bounded toward Lomaddis and the hostage he was dragging backward with him.

Lomaddis stumbled and mother jerked free. What a terrible sight must have confronted Lomaddis in the face of the raging Apache.

And then Manolete sprang. Fully upon Clete's chest he leaped like a cougar, and the two men crashed to the earth. A knife flashed and sank deep into Clete's chest. Like thunderbolts the blows fell, bone splintering and cracking beneath the blade.

"Katy!" mother yelled.

Skeels snatched me by the hair again and dragged me across the ground. Instead of pulling away, I twisted around and leaped at him and sank my teeth into his arm. He howled and flung me off.

"Katy! Away!" Mac boomed above Reba's thundering hooves.

I scrambled to the side.

Skeels whipped around. The most diabolical creature I had ever known was no coward. Sixgun in hand, he stood straight

and still, edge first, like a fencer. The Schofield roared and rocked and roared again.

I spun toward Mac. And then I saw it. I see it still. I always will.

Reba was on fire. Her eyes flashed like flares, her nostrils stretched wide, sucking in air. In the bright sunlight, every muscle was rippling and rolling like molten copper.

Mac sat tall in the saddle despite the gunfire. Then his right hand dropped to his left side, and when it rose again his saber was seated there. Higher it rose as he twisted his wrist and turned the tip forward—*in tierce point*. And then he closed at last on the man who vowed to destroy all that he loved. Skeels fired once more and gave no ground as the blade slashed down and Mac swept his head from his shoulders. It flew off and tumbled away down the slope, down a ravine, down into the cauldrons of Hell.

Mac reined about and sheathed his saber and swooped down on me. He scooped me up behind him and we rode to mother and Manolete.

I slipped from Reba and ran into mother's arms.

Skeels' horse wandered back, and I took him by the reins. All of us just stood there and breathed in God's fresh air.

After a few minutes, mother turned to Manolete.

"I'm so sorry," she said.

He read the guilt in her eyes, but I could see from his expression that he dismissed it as meaningless.

Skeels' horse jerked at the reins, and I followed his gaze as he looked down the valley.

"Oh, no," I said.

At least two dozen riders were heading straight for us from the pass at the far end of the valley.

"Skeels' men," mother said. "They'll kill us all."

With an eerie calmness, Mac dismounted. Then he lifted me into the saddle.

He picked up mother's sixgun and handed it to her. "Take

Skeels' horse," he said, and she mounted.

He looked at Manolete. "I can't ride that wild paint of yours," he lied. "On your horse."

Manolete stared at him. "My life is coming to an end." He looked at me and mother and then back at Mac. "Yours is not. Go."

"This is insane," mother said. "Katy can ride with me. We can all go."

"Too slow," Manolete said. "Go now. I will delay them."

"All right," Mac said.

He slipped off his medal of St. Michael and handed it to me. I put it on. Then he gently stroked Reba on the forehead and pressed his lips to the white star on her face.

He whispered, "Take care of my girl."

I was about to answer him when I realized he was speaking not to me but to Reba. He slid his carbine from the scabbard and then turned away and mounted the paint.

Manolete scooped a handful of cartridges from his horse's saddlebag and took his Winchester and reloaded it. Then he turned to face the horsemen racing up the valley. He never looked back at us again.

"Go!" Mac ordered, and we were off.

Despite her earlier exertions, Reba shot out of there like a bolt of lightning. She outdistanced mother's horse as if he were lame. I was closing on the pass through the mountains when I heard mother scream, "No!" I looked back over my shoulder. She had stopped a quarter-mile back and was watching the terrible unfolding.

Mac had never left. He stood side by side with Manolete. Each man held his carbine and waited for the killers to come.

I managed to turn Reba around. I raced back, squeezing my medal hanging from my neck. "Oh, Michael, please help them! Send them a legion of angels! Please don't let these men die."

Skeels' men were no fools. They split in two and began to circle. Still no shots had been fired. Mac and Manolete began to

pivot until they stood back to back, like doomed men, like valiant men—like Romans.

I pulled up by mother. She sat astride her horse and stared. Her face was the face of death.

"It's done," she said.

The explosion of gunfire seemed to shatter my skull. At least half the horsemen tumbled from their saddles.

I snapped to the right. Above the game trail on the ridge stretched a line of blue. Carbines roared again. More killers fell dead to the earth.

"My angels!" I yelled.

Most stood dismounted, but one man in four remained on his horse and held the reins of three others. Suddenly the rest leaped onto their steeds and the bugle sounded. They snapped into a column of fours and charged down the slope.

The hat flew from the lead officer, and I saw the silver hair of Colonel Hargrave. He was one with his men and one with his mount. Lean and taut and magnificent. He was honor, he was valor, he was America.

He was the United States Cavalry.

Saber in hand, he led the charge with Captain Colton beside him, and all the men's sabers flashed in the sunlight.

Suddenly the surviving killers remembered business elsewhere. They veered off and bolted up the valley toward the pass from which they had come.

The bugler sounded recall. The cavalry let them go. A year later, we learned that the bandits did reach Mexico, where they had a final and fatal rendezvous with the *rurales*.

Not waiting for mother, I raced back. My angels stood all in a line as if they were on a parade ground. Their horses snorted and twitched and swatted flies with their tails.

Colonel Hargrave dismounted. Still holding his saber, he approached his old friend and his old enemy.

"Colonel John Hargrave," Mac said, "this is Manolete of the Chiricahua Apache."

The colonel stopped ten feet in front him. He raised his saber vertically, hand before his chin, in salute to his former foe.

Manolete nodded.

"Sir," the colonel said, lowering his saber, "the United States government requests that you return to the agency at San Carlos. I will accompany you there myself, on my honor. I will answer for your safety, or die in the event."

"I will go," Manolete said, studying him with those eyes that looked both outward and inward at once. "And I will tell my children's children of you on this day."

We stayed in the Dragoons the remainder of the day. The colonel wanted to rest his men and mounts. They had been in the field a long time. He did send out scouting parties to see if any of Skeels' men were still around, but they were gone.

That night around the campfire still lives in me. Not a day passes without something igniting it in my mind. Some of my favorite moments were when Manolete recalled with a half-smile how often he and his men had eluded the soldiers, who sometimes had walked within feet of the Apaches. Sergeant Paddy Ryan roared with laughter at this. The younger troopers seemed puzzled by his good humor, but I knew that a tough old Irishman respected no one more than a man who had bested him.

Colonel Hargrave and Manolete spoke quietly together. I could catch only snatches of their conversation. I saw, though, by the colonel's manner that he was relishing this moment. Reading his memoirs many years later, I confirmed what I sensed around the fire, that this night formed the pivot point of his career. Not that he had "captured" the Infamous Manolete—though foolish journalists later made that claim. Rather, that here, in the Dragoons, two old foes treasured the fact that they could share more than anyone else would dare imagine. When his book describes his later years as a staff officer, one can see the recounting of that to be merely a formality. Jack Hargrave is sixty-one years old now and long retired. He still writes to me two or three times a year. I cherish those letters. In them, his

thoughts often return to a precious night under the Arizona stars with the last of the great Apache chiefs.

I dreaded the ending of this night. After the conversation waned, Manolete stood and walked to the edge of the firelight. He stared off to the north, into the blackness. I had no idea what feelings pumped in that fathomless heart, but I had to go to him. He heard me long before I got there. He turned around and gazed down at me. I wanted to say something memorable. All I did was stand there with my lower lip quivering.

"Do not cry, Coloradita."

That brought the tears. I hugged him as tightly as I could and cried as hard as I can ever remember crying. I was sobbing by the time I was done. He stroked my hair and held me and said nothing. Silence is the great virtue of the Apaches. Finally he eased back a bit and looked down at me.

"Do not weep anymore, little one. The world is not so sad."

I nodded, but my throat was too clogged to say anything.

"Do you think, Coloradita, that we will meet again?"

I did not know what to say.

"We will," he said, smiling. His eyes glanced at the heavens. "Up there."

I bit my lip.

"Manolete will wait for you." He reached down and brushed away the last of my tears.

I felt mother's hand on my shoulder. I looked up at her. She said nothing but just gazed at me with love. I turned back to Manolete. He nodded. As I backed away, I took his right hand, and his strong fingers slid through mine for the final time.

I sat by the fire and just stared into the flames. I was beyond tears now. After a short time, I heard Mac get up. He joined Manolete standing at the edge of the firelight, and they spoke together. The flames only partly lit them. It was an eerie scene, as if they were straddling two worlds, but living only half in each. It seemed to be the story of their lives.

I could hear their tone but not what they said to one

another, and Mac never told me. But a different and far more profound knowledge was granted to me that night. In their intensity and earnestness, volumes were being spoken. Some of those Eastern do-gooders of whom Mac was so contemptuous would have said that these two men were at last recognizing their common humanity. I knew it was nothing of the sort. The cozy moralists in their tearooms were hopelessly lost, ignorant of the blood and death telling a different moral out here on the border with Crook. Colonel Hargrave, more subtle than the vacantly pious in their armchairs back East, knew better. He wrote that each man realized that the challenge of facing each other had helped make him the man that he had become. It was true right down to the core. And yet, there was more to it even than that.

It was not until a dozen years later that I came to know it. I was sitting alone on our front porch under a crescent moon and thinking again about that night. Not through any brilliance of thought did I come to it. I am certain it was revealed to me only through the beneficence of God. I saw in my mind Mac and Manolete again standing together in the half light, and then it struck like lightning across a black landscape. Each of these men at last comprehended not the other man, but the essence of himself. Across a battleground of pain and anguish and staggering valor they had reached the high ridge, the lookout point. The haze burned off and all was clear. As though each man was a mirror to the other, he saw in the man before him the fulfillment of his life. There, without a shred of arrogance, both of them finally grasped the full and lasting greatness of their own unconquerable totality.

21

"Tonight?" mother asked in surprise.

"Yes," I said

"I don't have time for that," she snapped. She continued folding the laundry.

"But we have to be there. Jim told me to tell you."

The people of our town were not always wise, but they were usually good and they were always generous. They had decided to give a dinner in tribute to A Troop for ridding them of the scourge of Skeels and his minions—and for convincing Manolete to return from his dangerous exile. Colonel Hargrave was already escorting Manolete to San Carlos with a single battalion, so Captain Colton was here with the rest of the troop to represent the regiment.

"What's wrong?" I asked.

"Does anything have to be?"

I just stared at her.

After a few minutes she looked up from the folded bed sheets. There must have been pain on my face, because she jumped up and crushed me to her.

"Oh, Katy, you're my one grip on sanity," she said, squeezing me even more tightly. "It's time for us to talk of adulthood."

I remained quiet.

"You know what a mile marker is, don't you?"

"Yes."

"Well, life has mile markers. Places where people take the measure of their lives. These markers appear before they realize, but they're times of reckoning. I don't know where they come from. Maybe God puts them there. Sometimes I think it's Satan who drives them into the ground. But they're there."

She paused to let me grasp that.

"It's when people reach these milestones that they make decisions. Like when your daddy died and I decided to buy the mercantile. Do you understand what I mean?"

"I think I do."

"When Mac's wife died, that was a marker. It wasn't long afterward that he decided to retire from the army. Probably he never even thought about what he'd do if she died, but when she did, that became a marker. A reason for change."

I must have looked confused.

"Everything that's happened here lately—with Mac and Lomaddis and Manolete and everything else—that's a marker, too. It's a conclusion." She pressed my fingers. "Katy, Mac will be moving on now."

"On? Do you mean to town?"

"Away."

"To where?"

"I don't know. But away from us."

"No!" I shouted. "Mac would never leave us!"

"No, he never will. He'll never leave our hearts. But his job is done now. He took us under his care when we needed him. But it's over. We can't—."

"No, no, no! You're wrong!"

"Scamp, he can't live in your bedroom forever. He knows that. He's always known it."

"Then he can live in town."

"Oh, sweetheart, I can't explain how I know what I know. I just do."

"No!" I shouted again.

Apacheria

Mother remained calm, but it was a sad calm. "Scamp, Mac is an Indian fighter. A scholar of sorts, too. Maybe even a kind of philosopher. The best kind. He's a tough and complex man, and he has a life separate from a widowed merc owner and her daughter."

My anger at mother fled as fast as it had come. I knew now that she had simply gone temporarily mad. This happened to middle-aged women sometimes.

"No, mommy, you're just wrong. *We're* Mac's life."

She released my hand and looked away. "I wanted to believe that for a spell. I still want to. But it's just a fairy tale I told myself. We can't live on fantasies. Either of us."

Mother should have been furious with me. An eleven-year-old's look of condescension is a terrible thing. But she just pulled me close and let me luxuriate in my own sense of superiority and wisdom. Naturally, it bothered me that she was so upset, but I knew it would soon pass. Mac was not going anywhere. How could he? *We* were here. His Fireball knew him far better than mother ever would.

The Paradise dining room was awash with more flags than on the Fourth of July. All the town notables and a random selection of ordinary folk had been invited. It was an open secret that Sheriff Blaine had come up with the idea. Yet if someone mentioned it to him, he changed the subject. I think he felt guilty about the offhand and cutting remark he had tossed at Mac about the regiment. One secret that was not so open, but that mother later revealed to me, was that Jim was paying half the food bill. How he managed that I still do not know.

A fascinating fact I learned that night was how uncomfortable, and even puzzled, most soldiers were with adulation. This was especially true of the enlisted men. It looked to me as if Paddy Ryan—whose rough-hewn letters to his sister

were later published and offer a gripping account of Indian fighting in Apacheria—would rather have been out somewhere dining on hardtack and horse thigh than on the choice cuts provided now by our finest citizens.

Fortunately for the sergeant, Captain Colton deflected most of the attention, especially that of the ladies.

It was funny seeing the occasional soldier slip his watch out and lay it in his lap so he could sneak a peek as the evening wore on. The president of our small cattlemen's association felt compelled to say a few words, which met with polite applause. Then he called on Jim to offer some remarks, and our sheriff looked like he had been cow kicked. But when others seconded the idea, he stepped reluctantly before the group.

Jim spoke for no more than two minutes, but he did so with such simple eloquence that there was no one who was not touched. He admitted that he had not always appreciated the United States Cavalry. But a special friend had corrected him. Now he said he saw with different eyes, and he had at last recognized the wisdom of an Arabian proverb he had read long ago. He said that when he saw an American trooper and his mount flying across the plain, he knew that it truly was the wind of Heaven that blew between a horse's ears.

As Jim stepped away, there was no applause, just hushed awe. Then the troopers exploded and the room rocked with their cheers.

I looked at Mac sitting across the table from me. He was not applauding. He was too stunned. Jim glanced at us as he made his way between the tables. He left shortly afterward.

Jim's casual remarks, unrehearsed and therefore so moving, formed the unexpected climax of the event. The dinner began to wind down after that.

Mother had seemed distracted, and even distant, all evening. If Mac had noticed, he acted as if he did not. He was cheerful and joshed me even more than usual.

Apacheria

When Captain Colton announced that it was time for A Troop to return to its barracks, mother actually looked afraid, as if the end of this night were the end of the world.

Mac made no effort to move, and we were the last people remaining in the dining room. He finished his coffee and looked at mother.

"Mary, there are some unspoken things that have to be discussed."

"Yes," she said.

"We've come to a marker in the road."

Mother said nothing.

I felt so bad for her. She seemed as fearful and helpless as a little girl with night terrors.

"Things have to change, Mary. I've enjoyed being a boarder at the Malone homestead. . . ."

"We've enjoyed it, too."

"But this can't go on."

"I know," she said in a raspy whisper.

"It isn't seemly. You have a reputation that—."

"I don't care about my reputation."

"I know that, but you have to think of Katy."

"But can't we change the rules? Just once?"

I had never heard mother plead before. That was how much agony she was in.

"No," Mac said. "We cannot. I'd rather take an arrow in the heart than see your character questioned. And besides, there are signposts in the road here. There are life changes that can't—."

"Oh stop it!" she said. "Don't you think I know that?"

Mac seemed puzzled by her anger. He reached for his hat and stood up. "Don't you know your boarder must take his leave?"

I stared at him in disbelief and felt as if I had been punched in the stomach. I was unable to breathe.

Mac looked down at mother and glanced over at me. Then he sailed his hat toward me. It landed sideways on my head.

He dropped to one knee. "Mary Malone, would you brighten the declining years of this old horse soldier by becoming Mrs. Redmond McGregor?"

I shrieked and jumped up and scattered dishes everywhere.

The pair of tears that ran down mother's face did not detract from her but sanctified her in her beauty. She reached out and took Mac's hand.

"Yes," she said with the full-throated assurance of the queen of my world.

Mac rose and so did she. Their arms encircled each other and she laid her head against his shoulder and the tears flowed. And there they stood, serene and silent in their love.

"When did you know?" mother said at last, still resting against him.

"From the moment you looked up from that ledger book. When Katy led me in by the hand."

"Oh, Red, don't tease me."

"From that very moment, Mary."

"But you were going to leave," I said. "You were going to go."

He smiled at me. "God—and Manolete—had other plans."

He held out his hand and I went over and he pulled me close to both of them.

"But there was one thing that had to happen first," he said to me. "Someone had to sneeze and I had to look over. And a freckled face had to smile at me as no little girl had ever smiled at me before." He gazed at mother. "Mary, I love you with all my heart, but I have to tell you that I loved the Fireball first."

Mother laughed and pulled me tight.

And now it was my turn to squeeze them both and anoint them with my tears.

22

There is more to tell, but I am spent. I must bring an end. Evening is coming on, and Tim is lighting the fire. I hear my girls playing outside, and soon it will be time for their baths.

If God wills, I will write more someday. For now, I wanted simply to tell the story of a man of war who brought lasting peace to a lonely young widow and her daughter. A man who, like a prophet of old, rode in unbidden out of the searing desert. And when an angel fluttered a tiny freckled nose, the man turned and saw a mission to fulfill. With eyes as blue as the heavens, he took it all in. And for a trusting little girl, he cast a gentle light on the most profound mysteries of humanity.

To my left on the desk, during the entire time I have composed this testament, has lain a buckskin shirt, still soft after all these years. Once it belonged to the best hated and most feared man in all Apacheria, who removed his own garment to clothe a shivering little girl. And who lives forever in my memory as a giant.

Another sacred relic, as meaningful to me as the medal of St. Michael around my neck, has rested at my right hand. It is a buff campaign hat, scarred by a dozen battles, the faded yellow cord restored now to its rightful place around the crown. In my moments of unease, a glance in its direction settles me. At times of great fear or sorrow or longing, I lay my hand upon it, and

comfort and strength flow to me in a manner beyond reason. Then am I at peace again.

Night is falling. I am smiling because in the distance I hear the whistle of a train racing through the darkness and carrying people to Heaven.

And, like the messengers in *The Book of Job*, I have survived to tell *thee*.

www.ingramcontent.com/pod-product-compliance
Ingram Content Group UK Ltd.
Pitfield, Milton Keynes, MK11 3LW, UK
UKHW041450180426
11946UKWH00013B/144/J